FINDING MITCH

LYNN JAXON

COPYRIGHT

The following story contains sexual situations and strong language. It is intended for adult readers.

PROLOGUE

Ten years earlier
~Mitch~

The bell echoes throughout the halls. Hoots and hollers can be heard as the doors burst open, the seniors making a show of waving to the building, some flipping it the bird. Today is the last day of class. Two weeks until graduation. I have mixed feelings. On one hand, I'm excited to be graduating and moving on to college, but on the other, I don't want this to end. I'll be going to the University of Arkansas, and Jayna, my girlfriend, is headed to Harvard. I'm so proud of her. She is our class valedictorian, and I'm the salutatorian. I'll give the opening remarks at graduation, and she'll give the big speech about our lives just starting, being productive members of society, blah, blah, blah. Better her than me.

Yes, we are *that* couple. Where you see one, you see the other. We were prom king and queen, voted most likely to succeed, most likely to get married, et cetera. I guess you can say we are *the* couple of Westwood High. We've been together since sophomore year, just like my parents, Benson and Emily Davis. Unlike most teens, my parents believed in young love. Nothing can tear them apart. I hope to be just like them one day. I have to believe Jayna and I will be able to survive time and distance.

I'm startled from my thoughts when Jayna jumps into my arms.

"We did it, baby. Our high school days are over."

Placing her back onto the ground, I turn and squat down so she can jump onto my back. "You ready for your ride?" She loves when I carry her around. I love it, too. Having her long legs wrapped around me makes my dick harden.

"I'm always ready to ride you." She gives me a wink. I don't miss her double meaning, but there's one problem. We haven't had sex yet.

We decided to wait until we were eighteen before we took that step. Not that we haven't done some...exploring. Well, I turned eighteen in April, and she turned eighteen on Tuesday. She knows I have something planned, but doesn't know what or when. I'm going to take her to an inn and spa on the lake. I've been working at my dad's gym, EM Fitness, and saving for this night for over a year. I already have her bag in the back of my truck.

As we near my vehicle, Jayna hops down. I pull her into a scorching kiss that will probably get us in trouble if a teacher sees. When I finally pull away, we're both panting.

"Oh, how I missed those lips. Seven hours is just too long to go without kissing you."

She lightly slaps my chest. "Silly boy. I think you survived."

"Just barely. How were finals?" I ask.

Laughing, she blows on her knuckles and rubs them on her shoulder. "Piece of cake."

I smile. "I never doubted it for a minute."

"What about you, stud?" Jayna teases, coming up with the nickname once I started working out after work.

"You think I'm a stud?" I grin and waggle my eyebrows.

Before she can comment, the gang rushes up, slapping their hands on the hood of my truck.

"What's up, bro!" Jeff shouts, giving me a fist bump. "You two coming to the party at Eddie's tonight?"

Jayna looks at me expectantly. "Sounds like fun."

"Not tonight, boys. My girl and I have other plans."

A surprised look crosses her face. "You didn't tell me we had plans."

"If I told you, it wouldn't have been a surprise, would it?"

"Where are we going?" Her brow furrows, probably trying to figure out if I've left any hints.

Eddie bumps my shoulder with his. "I'll catch you later, man. You two lovebirds have fun. Don't do anything I wouldn't do."

I snort. "That doesn't leave me much room, does it?" Eddie is the school player. He does plenty that I would never dream of. "Catch ya later. Don't get too wasted tonight."

"Psh, is that even possible?" he retorts.

"Davis is finally going to do the deed," teases Jeff.

I shove his shoulder. "Watch your mouth, asshat! Unlike you, some of us aren't controlled by our dick...let alone announce it."

Jeff's girlfriend, Jamie, swats his arm and glares at him. "Don't be an ass, Jeff. Sorry, guys. He has no filter. Have fun this weekend. Call me Monday, Jayna. We can get together and go shopping for an outfit for graduation."

After they walk away, I pull Jayna to me and whisper into her ear, "Now, where were we?"

She giggles. "You were just about to tell me where you're taking me."

"Oh, you think so?" I pull her body even closer, letting her feel the evidence of what I'm thinking. "I thought you were just about to kiss me and make me love drunk."

She licks her lips, making my dick even harder. Knowing exactly what she's doing, she turns and climbs into the truck, looking over her shoulder. "Let's get out of here first, then I promise to make you love drunk."

I all but sprint around to my side of the truck. This is what I've been dreaming about for three years.

Once I pull out of the parking lot, her hand finds mine. I squeeze it gently, bringing it to my lips. "I love you, Jayna. Are you ready for this?"

"I love you more. And I've *been* ready. I can't wait to see what you have planned."

When I drive past her street, she turns to me. "Don't I need to get stuff from my house? What about my parents? Do they know your plans?"

"So many questions." I let out a chuckle. "Look in the back seat. I already have your suitcase packed. Your mom packed it as your dad gave me a lecture that I'd better be *safe,* glaring at me the whole time." I snort. "That was an awkward conversation."

When I finally told her parents my plans, I was sweating bullets. I thought I had nerves of steel, but evidently telling your girlfriend's dad you're taking her away for the weekend will make even the strongest men queasy.

"You think of everything, Mitch. Thank you for doing this for me...for us. My parents love you, and they know how much you love me. Besides, I'm eighteen now. There really isn't much they can say." She chuckles. "Hell, my mom got pregnant with me when she was sixteen, so that would be the pot calling the kettle black. They just want us to be extra careful."

"I assured them we were covered."

"My mom knows I'm on the pill, she took me to the doctor when I was sixteen, but I told her when we decided the time was right, we'd use extra protection. That seemed to put her mind at ease."

"You know, we can just relax and spend time together in the hot tub. We don't have to do anything you're not ready for."

"There's a hot tub?" She bounces excitedly in her seat. "Where are you taking me?"

Tapping my finger on my lips, I give her a sly grin. "Hmm... Should I tell you now or make you wait?"

"You love me, so you should tell me."

"That I do, beautiful. Okay..." I pause, waiting for her reaction. She doesn't disappoint when she bounces a little again. "We're going to the Inn & Spa at Vista Ridge."

She gasps. "Are you serious? That must've cost you a fortune."

"Baby, you are worth every penny. I've been saving up, but my parents pitched in so we could do some of the extras that are offered."

She gives me a beautiful smile, a single tear running down her face.

* * *

Jayna sucks in a breath when we pull up to the inn. I must admit, it's beautiful. Patting myself on the back, I smirk inwardly...or so I thought.

"What are you smirking about over there?"

"Busted... I was just thinking how good I did finding this place." I'd looked online for hours to find just the perfect spot. This resort was just built last year.

"You definitely scored some major boyfriend points."

Putting the truck in park, I climb out and run around to the passenger side, opening Jayna's door. I help her down, then we walk hand in hand into the building.

"Let's get checked in so we can get our weekend started." My heart rate spikes in anticipation of what's to come. I hope I don't make a fool out of myself.

The girl at the desk gives me a flirty smile and asks for my name. I give her that, as well as my reservation number.

She types on her computer. "This room has already been taken care of. Do you want to use the same credit card for incidentals? I'll just need to see your driver's license."

I nod as I pull out my wallet and hand her my license and credit card. My parents told me to get one as soon as I turned eighteen so I could start building my credit. It only has a five-hundred-dollar limit, but it's good to have.

She looks at my driver's license and back to me, smiling seductively and pushing my receipt and keycard forward. "Thank you, Mr. Davis. Let me know if I can be of any service to you while you're here. You'll be staying in building number two, second floor, room two twenty-eight. Your room number is on your keycard."

Glancing at Jayna, I see her eyes narrowed and nostrils flared. You can practically see steam billowing out of her ears. I turn back to the clerk. "I'm sure me and my girlfriend have everything we need." I put my hand on the small of Jayna's back and guide her back out to the truck before she can say anything. My girl can be quite the firecracker when provoked.

"What the hell, Mitch? I was going to give *Miss Let Me Know If I Can Be Of Any Service* a piece of my mind. Her tone and look she gave you told me exactly what kind of *service* she was talking about."

"Are you jealous?" I smile. "I like it. It's turning me the hell on."

"Of course I'm jealous. Look at you. A woman at least ten years older than you is hitting on what's *mine*! There isn't a woman alive who wouldn't be jealous."

I pull her to me so she can see how hard I am. I nibble on her ear. "I'll let you take that frustration out on me as soon as we get to our room."

Smiling, her anger fades. "Well... What are we waiting for?" She jumps into the truck before I can open the door for her.

Smirking, I climb in, seeing her flushed expression. I can't wait until she sees what's waiting for her in the room.

It takes all of two minutes to drive around to our building. "Here we are, Jayna. Right on the lake."

She sighs. "This is beautiful. I can't wait to see inside."

"Don't move. Let me open the door for you. This weekend is all about you."

An unwelcome thought crosses my mind. *How many more weekends are we going to have together? We will both be going off to college soon.*

I quickly school my features before I get to her door.

Jayna startles me by jumping into my arms. "Whoa, woman. I could've dropped you."

"Are you calling me fat?" She pokes me in the ribs, hard.

"Ouch! I'd never call you fat, Jayna. You are absolutely perfect."

She kisses me on the nose. "I know. I just love messing with you."

"Let me grab our bags." I set her down and open the back door. Her bag is twice as heavy as mine. I hook my duffle bag onto the handle of her rolling suitcase so I can pull them both. "Damn. What in the world did your mom pack in here?"

"Don't ask me. Knowing Mom, she made sure to pack what I'd need and then some."

"I'd say," I tease as we walk into the building.

Once the elevator doors close, Jayna pulls me into a heated kiss. After several minutes, she finally pulls away, panting. "I've always wanted to do that. It is so romantic when people kiss in an elevator."

The doors open, and with a bow, I gesture for her to go first. "Our room awaits, m'lady." We grasp each other's hand as we walk down the hall.

I wonder if her heart is beating as fast as mine. Will she like what I have set up? Mom promised me she would love it. Taking a deep breath, I insert the keycard into the door.

If Jayna's gasp is any indicator, then I did good. The room glows with the flickering of several battery-operated tea lights placed around. The white comforter on the king-sized bed is covered in red rose petals. A tray of fruit sits on the table, along with a fondue pot full of chocolate and a dozen red roses.

"Oh, Mitch...," she breathes out. "I'm speechless. How did you manage this?"

"You've met my mom, right? She gave me some pointers, but it was mostly my doing. She just made sure it was ready."

She throws her arms around me. "I love you! This is perfect."

She's right. It is perfect, but not because of the room. Because she's here with me. I know we're young, but as long as she's by my side, I would be happy anywhere. Leaning in, I capture her lips with mine, starting what turns out to be the greatest weekend of my life.

CHAPTER 1

Present Day
~Mitch~

"Thanks for nothing, asshole! You weren't that good anyway."

She picks up my shoe and hurls it at my head just before she slams the door to my apartment. Note to self: Don't leave your shoes near the door. Lila...or was it Lexi...knew the score when we left the club. Why do these women think that any guy who picks them up at a bar wants more than one night? I can't believe she got so pissed. I thanked her for a fun time and offered to call her an Uber. What more did she want? I'll give her this, though. She definitely knew how to use her mouth.

I startle when my cell starts to ring. It's two o'clock in the morning. Who the hell is calling me right now?

I walk around slowly, trying to figure out where it's coming from. Finally pinpointing the location, I dig around in the couch cushions, pulling it out. Henry's name flashes on the screen. Figures.

"What the hell, Henry? Do you know what time it is?"

"Five in the afternoon. Are you drunk or something?"

"You're in Australia, dumb ass. Did you forget about the time difference?"

"Shit, man. I'm sorry. Did I wake you up?" Before I can answer, he continues. "I have news I just couldn't wait to share with you. Kristi is pregnant! We're having a baby! Can you believe it? I'm going to be a daddy."

I smile, feeling his excitement coming through the phone. "Well, I'll be a damned. I'm gonna be an uncle? Congratulations, bro. I was beginning to think your little swimmers didn't work. You've been married for almost four years. After Emily was born, I could see how much Kristi wanted a baby, and y'all weren't even married yet. I guess this will be one vacation you'll never forget. What did Dad say?"

"What do you think? He cried like a baby. Marley had to take the phone away from him."

Our dad is such a softie. He's going to be an amazing grandfather.

Thinking about everything he's gone through up to this point, I wish I could bring myself to open my heart like he has. I still have flashbacks of the broken man he was six years ago after cancer took our mother. He was a shell of a man. Even though he found love again with Marley, I'll never allow myself to be that vulnerable and open to heartbreak. Fuck that. That's why I became a divorce lawyer. Love never lasts.

"Earth to Mitch. You still there?"

"Shit. I'm sorry. I was just thinking about Dad. He is going to spoil that baby rotten, just like he's spoiled our little sister. Little Emily will think she has a living and breathing doll to play with."

"Don't you know it. I can't believe she'll be five in just a couple months. Time sure does fly."

I try to stifle my yawn, unsuccessfully. "Sorry, man. It's just after two in the morning here and I'm beat. The chick I just sent packing was wild as hell."

"You sent someone home? At this hour? You're such an ass."

I laugh. "That's exactly what she said when she threw my shoe at me on her way out the door."

"Man, when are you going to stop the womanizing and settle down. You can't keep living like this."

"Not all of us want to turn in our Man Card and settle down."

"I'm going to tell Kristi you said that."

In the background, I can hear Kristi yelling something. I can't tell what, but I have a feeling I'm in trouble. She's like a sister to me. We became close when she moved in with Henry and me my last year of law school. I've missed her smart ass since moving to Dallas.

"Thanks for getting me in trouble, shithead."

"You do a bang-up job of that all by yourself. I love you, Mitch. We'll fly up to Dallas to see you one weekend after we get back. Kristi is dying to go shopping in the big city."

"Sounds like a plan. I love you, too. Give Kristi my love. She's going to be an amazing mother."

"Look at you, kissing up. You know she can't kick your ass all the way from here, so you're good. Talk to ya later."

I can't help but feel a little envious of what Henry and Kristi have. I hope they are an exception to the rule and are able to stand the test of time. It's hard to believe I actually thought I'd have that life. I was definitely a fool.

* * *

My alarm goes off what seems like only minutes later. I groan. *Shit...* I have a damn associate's Sunday breakfast at the country club. I hate going to these stupid things, but it's necessary if I want to become a partner someday. Maxon Burns started grooming me the second I got hired at the firm fresh out of law school. Said he liked my fire and determination. Called me the firm's "rainmaker". My good looks have definitely added to that status. Women wanting to divorce their rich husbands tend to flock to me in droves. They're disappointed when they learn I'd never risk my license by dating a client.

I shower, dress, then jump into my silver BMW i8. This car is my baby. Nothing like riding with the sunroof open and radio blasting to take your mind off of your troubles. This car set me back a pretty penny, though. I need to make junior partner soon. I try to live off of my earnings, not the inheritance I received after my mother passed away.

As much as I want to keep on driving past the country club, have a day to myself, I pull in and toss the valet my keys, my glare conveying I'd better not see a hint of a scratch on it when I come back out.

As soon as I enter the private dining room, I can hear Maxon's obnoxious laugh. Seeing me, he stands and gestures me over. "Speak of the devil... Get over here, Mitch."

Looking around the table, I realize that none of the other associates are here, only the senior partners–Burns, Toone, and Jefferson. I school my face to keep the surprise from showing. Sweat starts to form on my brow. I scroll through my memory to see if there's anything I've done that may have warranted this meeting. My record is exemplary. I've gotten my clients everything they've asked for in their divorce cases, sometimes more.

"Hello, gentlemen. Am I early?"

"Take a seat, Mitch. Everyone else received emails stating the brunch has been canceled for this month. We wanted to meet with you alone. All your hard work and no bullshit attitude have not gone unnoticed by the firm."

My heart rate increases and palms start to sweat. This is what I've been working for. I shrug, trying to act nonchalant. "I love to win. What can I say?"

Laughter rolls around the table. "Those words sound like money to me." Samuel Toone raises his glass, which appears to be scotch. It's not even noon.

Maxon clears his throat. "The reason we're here is to talk about one of the biggest cases we've handled in a long time. We want you to be lead counsel. If you win, we want you to join us as a junior equity partner. How does Burns, Toone, Jefferson, and Davis sound to you? With your record of success, we see you becoming a senior partner in no time."

"I'm honored. Tell me about this case."

Spencer Jefferson is the first to speak up. "Mitch, this one is big. Justin Taylor, of Taylor Oil, is being sued for divorce by his wife, Mitzie, citing adultery. He adamantly denies this and states *she* is the one who has been cheating."

I can see the media circus surrounding this one already. I just hope we are on the right side of the circus. "Who are we representing?"

"Mr. Taylor. We will have to pull out all the stops on this case, Mitch. Mr. Taylor hired a private investigator months ago when he first suspected Mitzie was cheating. Too many weekend *girlfriend* trips to suit him. We have a lot of evidence to substantiate his claims. What we don't know is if she has anything on him. He swears he has nothing to hide, but we can't be blindsided."

"I'm ready for this. There's no doubt in my mind I can pull off the win."

Mr. Burns slaps me on the back so hard I almost fall forward into the table. "And that's why you're here, son. Do us proud. Now, who's ready to eat?"

For the next hour, we eat and talk about some of our other cases. I'm still stunned at the turn of events. Henry will not believe it when I tell him about this. I know Mom is smiling down on me. She was so proud that I was going to become a lawyer.

I get another round of slaps on the back as we exit the private dining room. When I walk outside, the valet rushes to get my car, then hands me my keys as I hand him a tip. Time to go celebrate.

* * *

Hitting the hands-free button on the steering wheel, I call my best friend, Luke, to see if he wants to go hit the gym, then go out to our favorite bar. My body buzzes with adrenaline right now. I definitely need to hit the gym and work some off.

Three rings later, the phone connects. "Hey, man. How was your meeting?" He laughs. "Did you get in all your ass kissing for the month?"

"Ha-ha. Very funny. Actually, *they* were the ones doing the ass kissing. You happen to be speaking to the future junior partner of Burns, Toone, and Jefferson. Once I reach it and turn that junior partner status into senior partner in a few years, go ahead and add my name to that."

"Shut the fuck up. Are you serious?"

"Serious as a week with no sex. They told me if I win the next case, the partnership is mine. I'm so amped. I don't know what to do with all this energy. Do you want to hit EM Fitness, then go out and celebrate?"

"You know I'm game. I'll throw on some gym shorts and meet you there in about thirty. Will that work?"

"Sounds great. I'm headed home to change. I'll meet you there."

* * *

In no time, I head back out the door and drive to the gym. I smile as the clouds break and a beam of sunlight shines through the sunroof onto my face. I know it's my mom smiling down on me.

Kissing my fingers, I lift my hand through the opening. "I owe it all to you, Mom. You made me be the best I can be. I promised you I'd be successful, and it's finally happening." I sigh. "I'm just sorry I've failed you in the relationship department. I'll never have what you and Dad did. It's just not in the cards."

A few minutes later, I pull into the parking lot, Luke right behind me in his jacked-up Ford F-250. For the life of me, I can't figure out why he has to drive that monster. I've told him women are going to think he's compensating for something.

Climbing out of my car, I see him singing and bobbing his head to the music blaring from his truck.

I've never been able to get into Hank Jr. or David Allan Coe, but he listens to it like it's the greatest music in the world.

"How in the hell can you still hear with that crap blasting?" I yell. "I think people back in Arkansas can hear this shit."

He smirks, cupping his hand to his ear. "What'd you say?"

"Shut up, asshole. You ready to go hit it hard?"

We grab our bags and walk in. The gym is packed with too many people just hanging out and talking, taking up space. I need to remember to mention this to Dad when I call him later and tell him my news. He would never put up with people holding up the equipment while others are trying to use it. I don't feel right throwing my name around, even though Dad would love it if I did.

Benson Davis has turned EM Fitness into a household name. He named the gym after Mom, working his ass off to make a good life for us all.

Luke turns to me. "Where did all these people come from? Hell, none of them are even working out."

Just when I'm about to respond, two smoking hot chicks saunter up to us. On a scale of one to ten, they're both a twelve...until they open their mouths.

"Oh, my god! How'd you get so many muscles? Can I touch them?"

Is this girl serious? "Excuse me?" I look at Luke, who's fighting back a laugh, then back at her. "This is a gym. You know, the place you go to *get* big muscles."

The blonde with the big tits raises her arms, pushing her hands through her hair, causing her crop top to raise over her sports bra. "I'll bet the muscles I can't see are big, too. I'd love for you to demonstrate just how *hard* your body is."

With that, Luke can't hold back anymore and almost falls to the floor laughing, tears running down his face.

Blonde number one scowls and throws her head back. "Come on, Brandi. It's obvious these two have no taste." She pulls on her friend's arm and they storm off.

I shove his shoulder. "Did you have to laugh so hard. I could've gotten laid and not even had to work for it."

"Dude, just listening to her killed my brain cells. You *do* want to win that case, don't you? She'd be a liability."

She may have been a bit of an airhead, but she was smoking hot. "You know my rules. I don't go back for seconds, so one night wouldn't have killed too many brain cells."

"You are such a man whore. How are you and your brother even related?"

I waved my hand through the air. "My brother is a love-struck fool. I want no part of that shit."

"You will someday. Mark my words."

"You're one to talk. I don't see you dating anyone."

"I may not be in a serious relationship, but I don't have your one-and-done rule. If it's good, I have no problem going back for seconds."

He smirks. "How about we hit the treadmill so you can run off that semi you're sporting?"

I throw my towel at his face and we hit the treadmill.

After a three-mile run on an incline, I'm done. I look over, seeing Luke already heading to the water fountain, but I doubt it's for a drink. Tabitha, one of the workers he's been flirting with for the past few months, stands there, cleaning cloth in hand. She just smiles shyly at him. It makes him crazy that she doesn't fall all over herself when he talks to her.

When she sees me, she smiles politely. "Hi, Mr. Davis. Did you have a good workout?"

"I told you to call me Mitch, Tabitha. Mr. Davis is my dad."

She blushes, looking at the floor. "Sorry, Mitch. I...I have to get back to work." At that, she hurries away like her ass is on fire.

Luke places his hands on his hips, watching her. "What the hell, man? I can't even get her to talk to me."

"That's because she likes you. I'm her boss's son, so she feels like she *has* to talk to me."

"We both know that's bullshit. Let's go do upper body, then call it a day."

"Sounds good to me. I'm looking forward to a shower, drinks, and a hot, willing woman in my bed tonight."

CHAPTER 2

~Mitch~

The line outside Big D's stretches around the block. But because I represented the owner in his divorce and kept him from losing half of his club, I've been listed for immediate entrance any time I want. That was an ugly case. Not only was his ex-wife skimming money from the club and putting it into a secret account, she was cheating with one of the bartenders and got pregnant. She had told him at the beginning of their relationship that she didn't want kids, so he didn't bother to tell her he probably couldn't father children anyway because of a football injury in college. When he confronted her, she pulled the *but I'm having your baby* card. That was the nail in the coffin. We served her papers the next day. She didn't have a leg to stand on when his doctor testified that he was indeed sterile. That, as well as the evidence he had of her stealing, pretty much left her with next to nothing. She's lucky we didn't countersue for what she did.

Reason number billion and one why I don't believe in love.

Luke hits me on the shoulder, bringing me out of my thoughts. "Damn. Look at all these sexy women. If you don't find a piece of ass tonight, then you've lost your touch."

As we walk in, the sound of the country music is deafening. You can almost feel the floors vibrating to the beat of the music. Walking through the crowd to the bar takes forever. I hope there's not a fire or we're all in trouble.

"What can I get you boys?" the sexy bartender purrs.

"Luke, you want a beer, or something hard?"

He smirks at the bartender. "Give me whatever house brew you have on tap. I've already got something...*hard.*"

She rolls her eyes at that comment and looks at me.

"I'll take the same."

As she walks two steps away to draw our beers, I look her up and down. "Damn, you are one fine lady. Better make it an extra frosty glass, because the heat coming off of you will make my beer warm."

I hear her snort as she sets our glasses down and walks away to take another order.

Luke laughs loudly. "That, my friend, was corny, even for you. You'll be lucky if she doesn't spit in your next beer."

"Whatever, man. I saw her blush when I said it. Besides, you're the one who said, 'I've already got something hard.' Seriously?"

Just as Luke is about to respond, we're both hit with the fragrance of strong perfume and look up to see a petite redhead sit on the stool next to Luke. As cute as she is, I don't sleep with redheads. They make me think of my mom, which is just creepy. I'll let Luke have her. I take a long draw of my beer to watch the show.

"Well... Hello there, gorgeous," Luke says.

She licks her lips and breathlessly replies, "Hello yourself." Propping her arms on the bar, she squeezes her fake tits together to make them pop out of her low-cut blouse.

I hear a hum of appreciation from Luke. "Can I buy you a drink, darlin'?"

"I'd love one, and you can call me Zee."

"Zee? Interesting name. Is that your real one?"

"It's what all my friends call me."

I turn back toward the bar, tuning them out, locking eyes with the hot bartender. She smiles and brings me another beer. Damn, I didn't even realize I had finished the first one. Her blonde hair is pulled up on top of her head, tendrils falling into her face. I can picture them caressing my dick when she takes me into her mouth. Shit, I'm getting hard just thinking about it.

I gain control of myself and ask, "What time do you get off tonight?"

"Ten. I'm just covering a few hours for a co-worker. She should be here..." She looks down at her watch, "in less than an hour."

Just as I'm about to respond, Luke stands and leans down toward my ear. "Hey, man. I'm out. I'm taking Zee home. Don't do anything I wouldn't do." He pats me on the shoulder and leads the redhead to the door. She doesn't know what's in store. He is one kinky motherfucker.

When I turn back to the bar, I see the bartender helping someone else. Then I glance down a napkin in front of me, writing scrawled on it.

Wait for me. I'm up for a good time if you are. Xox Molly.

Oh, hell yeah. Looks like both Luke and I are getting lucky tonight.

Several minutes later, nursing my third beer, I feel a woman's arms wrap around my neck and the whisper of her hot breath against my skin. "Dance with me, sexy."

I spin around on the barstool, seeing Molly standing there, and pull her close. "Baby, I'll dance with you, then I'll make you sing my name."

Her hard nipples poke through her lace bra, which is visible in her tight white t-shirt she had on under the apron she's no longer wearing. She looks delicious in her tight jean skirt and see-through shirt.

"I don't even know your name," she pants.

I wink. "Mitch."

We head onto the dance floor, Conway Twitty's "I'd Love to Lay You Down" coming on. I sing and grind into her ass, feeling her breathing accelerate. When I spin her around to face me and pull her close, her chest rubbing against mine, I know she can feel the evidence of my attraction as I continue to grind into her.

"I wanna fuck you hard," I whisper into her ear and bite her on the neck. "Do you want that?"

"Yes," she all but moans.

"Where do you live?" I hope it's close. My dick is straining against my jeans.

"Just down the road. You can drive. I'll pick up my car tomorrow."

I all but drag her out of the bar and to my car. Her eyes grow wide when she sees my BMW i8.

"Screw going home. I want you to fuck me in this car. Pull into the employee lot in the back. Nobody should be leaving or arriving any time soon."

As soon as we're in the car, she pulls her shirt over her head, then reaches over and unbuttons my jeans, freeing me. I'm glad I went commando tonight. I practically come off the seat when she leans over and licks the precum from the tip of my dick.

"Do you have a condom?"

"In the glove box," I rasp out as she takes me into her mouth. Now this is my kinda girl. She is shameless and not afraid to go for what she wants. As long as she only wants tonight, all is good.

I can barely shift gears to get us to the back parking lot. She's giving the girl from the other night a run for her money in the suction department.

I park quickly, then lean my head back. "Oh baby, that feels so good. Take me all the way. I want to feel your teeth scraping my cock."

Those words seem to turn her on even more as she takes me all the way down. "Fucking hell!" I scream out as she swallows me down. She doesn't even have a gag reflex. I wrap her hair in my hands to guide her faster on my cock until I'm about to blow my load.

"Stop," I growl, pulling her mouth from my cock with a loud *pop*.

I lean the seat all the way back. "Get over here," I say, desire in my voice.

When she straddles me, her skirt goes up around her hips, baring her smooth, glistening pussy. Holy hell. Looks like I'm not the only one going commando tonight.

"You are so fucking wet. I want to taste you."

She crawls up, straddling my face, her knees on the almost non-existent back seat, and grasps the back headrest. As she lowers herself, I lick up her thighs, causing her to shiver. When I suck on her hard nub, she screams, "Oh, Mitchy!"

I still, feeling like a glass of cold water has been thrown into my face. Only one other person has called me that.

Molly doesn't seem to notice that my excitement has lessened as she explodes.

Breath eventually calming, she shimmies back down into my lap, reaching over to the glove box and grabbing a condom. My heart may not be in this, but my dick hasn't received the message and is still eager.

She rolls on the condom, then leans in for a kiss. Instead, I turn my head to the side and bite her shoulder. Kissing is too intimate. I haven't kissed a woman in years.

"Turn around and hold on to the steering wheel. You're going to need it," I command.

"Yes, sir."

She doesn't hesitate. I lick my lips. She has one plump and delicious ass. My hands squeeze both her ass cheeks and slam her down onto my hard cock, making her scream out.

"Yes! Fuck me hard!"

And that is exactly what I do. It doesn't take her long to detonate around me. With her pulsing muscles squeezing me, I let go with a hiss.

Molly smiles over her shoulder, panting. "Wow. Just wow. You are amazing. When can we do this again?"

I lift her off of me and place her into the passenger seat. "Baby, I don't do seconds. You were phenomenal, but tonight is it." I feel like an ass, but she was the one who initiated this.

It takes a minute for my words to register. When they do, she looks pissed. "Are you fucking *kidding* me?"

I shake my head. "I never led you to believe it would be more than just a fuck. Do you want me to take you home?"

"Fuck you," she spits and pulls her shirt back over her head, then climbs out of the car. "I can take myself home. You weren't that good anyway!"

With that, she slams the door and stomps off. A few seconds later, I hear the squeal of tires as she peels out of the parking lot.

CHAPTER 3

~Jayna~

It's hotter than hell in Texas, but I'm excited for the change. As I climb out of the Uber, I pull over the large box containing some medical books and family pictures. You'd think the driver would offer to help carry them in, but he barely even acknowledged that we had reached our destination. I look around at the sidewalk packed with business professionals and shoppers in their own world. The noise of horns honking and cars driving by is almost overwhelming. I've been practicing in a small town in Pennsylvania for the past two years. This is all so new to me.

I'm knocked out of my thoughts when what can only be described as a herd of dogs runs into me, their leashes wrapping around my legs.

"Oh, my god. I'm so sorry," pants the woman being pulled down the street by the five small and two large dogs. Why in the hell would anybody take on that many dogs at one time?

"It's fine." I chuckle, disentangling myself from the leashes. "Be careful, or they'll drag you into traffic."

"I'm good," she yells as they drag her up the sidewalk. "They know it's grub time when they get back home."

"You gonna get your stuff out of my car or what? I've got other people to pick up," the pimple-faced Uber driver says. He looks barely old enough to drive, but he's getting an attitude with me?

I frown and struggle to drag the box out of the car.

"Here. Let me help you."

When I hear the familiar, masculine voice behind me, I stiffen, goosebumps climbing up my back.

Sucking in a deep breath, I turn and look up into the unforgettable green eyes of Mitch Davis. Of all the people in the world, why is the first one I see the man I loved more than anything in the world? The same man who broke my heart. It takes everything in me to not climb back into the car and run away.

"Hi, Mitch."

"Jayna?" he asks, a look of shock and wonder on his face. "What in the world are you doing in Dallas?"

"I could ask you the same thing."

"Get your shit out of my car!" yells the Uber driver.

"Hold your ass, man! Is that any way to speak to a woman?" Mitch yells back and throws him a twenty. "Here. For your time."

Mitch picks up the box, sets it down on the sidewalk, and slams the car door. "Where are you headed?"

"My office is in the Hartford Towers." I tilt my head to the beautiful, forty-five story building to my left.

"No *shit?* My firm's in that building, too. We occupy the fortieth floor. What floor are you on?"

"The second, with all the other medical offices."

"It's good to see you...," we both say at the same time.

The song "Something People Say" by Rachel Wammack goes through my mind, along with all the hurt from the past.

There was a time we always took the words right out of each other's mouths.

When he reaches toward my face, almost like he can't stop himself, I back into one of the planted trees that line the sidewalk in this upscale part of downtown.

Mitch shakes his head slightly and picks up the box. "I'm sorry. Come on. I'll buy you a coffee. There's a Starbucks on the first floor, along with several other cafés and gift shops."

"Good to know. This is my first time at the building. I just flew in yesterday. All our stuff..." I swallow. *Fuck.* "All my stuff was delivered to my apartment on Saturday. It looks like a war zone." Just saying those words makes me stiffen and think of a man I'd rather forget.

Of course, that doesn't go unnoticed by Mitch, who furrows his brows. I never could get anything past him. "Are you okay?"

I laugh and try to blow it off. "Yeah. Just thinking of how much I have to do. Plus, I have patients coming in later." I look at my watch and see that it's almost nine. "What time do you need to be in the office?"

"Nine, but it's fine. Come on. Let me buy you a coffee. Do you still drink skinny mochas?"

My eyes widen. "You remember that?" I shouldn't be surprised. Mitch never forgets anything.

"I remember everything. You're hard to forget."

I don't know what to say to that. I study Mitch. He looks the same, yet different. There is a hardness about him that wasn't there when we last saw each other. It's that same hardness I remember hearing the last time I talked to him on the phone.

"I can't resist because, quite frankly, I'm addicted to Starbucks, thanks to your mom."

Mitch pauses a beat, then nods and walks toward the building, me following. As we walk inside, it makes me think about Emily, Mitch's mom, and how we always went to Starbucks before all his sporting events. Emily Davis was the sweetest woman I've ever met. She was like a second mother to me. It just killed me when I heard about her cancer after she had died. My parents did what they thought was best and didn't tell me Emily was sick. They knew I would leave and come running back home to comfort Mitch, even though he had asked for a "break" a year before and had been drifting further away from me. But what hurt me even more was how Mitch responded when I called. Subconsciously, I place my hand on my heart, remembering the pain and venom in his voice.

"Mitch, are you there?" I wait, just listening to his breathing on the other end of the line. "Are you okay? I just heard about your mom. I'm so sorry."

"What do you want, Jayna? Did you finally manage to find a minute to concern yourself with me? She's been dead for two weeks. Where were you then?"

"I didn't find out about it until today. We were out of the country on holiday. My parents didn't even tell me she was sick. I was furious with them, but they said they didn't want to ruin my holiday. I loved your mom. You know that. You know, you could've called, messaged, emailed, but you didn't. So it wasn't just my parents keeping me in the dark. I still love you, and it kills me that you are going through this."

An almost evil laugh comes through the phone. "Love? You love me? Fuck love. It doesn't exist. Love just causes pain and suffering. If you could see my dad right now, you'd know that love is not worth it.

"I need to go. Go back to your books and your friends and forget you ever knew me. I have no room in my heart for love."

It's been six years since that conversation, but it still hurts, a deep sadness enveloping me.

Mitch orders our drinks, and we walk to the end of the counter to wait. We both avoid making eye contact. I wonder if this is as hard for him as it is for me? Does he remember how horrible he was to me the last time we spoke?

"Mitch," the barista calls.

He grabs our coffee from the counter, handing me mine, then

walks to the bar to add sugar to his double shot espresso. I don't know how he drinks it without cream.

"Thank you, Mitch. I guess we'd better get going. I don't want you to be late because of me."

"It's fine, Jayna. If you hold my coffee, I can carry your box to your office."

We walk silently to the glass elevator. My cheeks heat, remembering the night we made love for the first time. We kissed the hell out of each other on the elevator on the way to our room before the best night of my life.

Mitch leans down and whispers, "Are you thinking about the same thing I'm thinking about?"

I have to get away from him, and quickly. I look over and see the ladies' room. "Do you mind if I run to the ladies' room really quick before we head up?"

"Sure. I'll wait over here." He points to a bench next to one of the marble columns.

I rush over to the bench and set down our coffee, then hurry into the bathroom and take a deep breath, looking at myself in the mirror. *I can do this.*

After a few minutes, regaining my composure, I walk back out into the lobby. I look up, seeing the man I've spent years missing, the pain so deep there aren't words to express it. But as I look closer, it's not the same man. This one's face is contorted in anger, eyes seemingly dead, spewing hateful words at the poor woman in front of him. Backing behind a column, I can't help but listen.

"What the *fuck* are you doing at my office? I told you, it was just one night. Don't call me. Don't text me. Don't write me a letter. You got off. I got off. We're even."

"Why are you being so mean? I thought we had something," she cries, wiping tears from her face.

"You knew the deal going in. I do believe my words to you were, 'Baby, this is just a one-night rodeo.' I'm sorry if you don't understand English."

"You're such an asshole!" she says, spins on her heel, and stomps out the door.

What the hell? How can this be the same man I once thought hung the moon?

I storm around the column and look at him with disgust. "What the hell was that? I can't believe what I just witnessed. How could you be so mean?"

Mitch smirks and shrugs. "I'm not the same man I was all those years ago, Jayna."

"No shit." I grab our coffee, which no longer has the appeal it did a few minutes ago, and stride to the elevator just as the doors open, Mitch following.

Riding up silently, I blow out a breath when the elevator doors open to the second floor. I'm about ready to lose it, and I refuse to let him see me break. "Just put the box there." I point to the floor. "I'll get it the rest of the way myself." I hold out his coffee.

"Jayna, don't be so dramatic. Let me carry it to your office."

"*I've got it,*" I growl.

By this time, the elevator starts buzzing because we've held open the doors too long. Mitch sets the box down in the hallway and backs away. He takes the coffee just before the doors shut.

"It was good to see you, Jayna. Maybe I'll see you around."

He almost sounds ashamed. Almost.

The morning goes by in a blur. I meet with the Human Resources manager, Charles, and the other staff, as well as get my office set up how I want it. My afternoon schedule is packed with patients having a wide range of medical issues, not allowing me time to think about my encounter with Mitch this morning.

Now that it's after hours, all the patients gone, the silence is welcome...until I start thinking about running into Mitch this morning and how he acted to that woman.

Of all the people to run into in this huge city, why did it have to be Mitch?

My heart starts to hurt when I think back to the day I left for Harvard.

Tears streaming down my face as Mitch and I stand in each other's arms, I can hardly get the words out. "I don't want to leave. Tell me to stay."

Using his thumbs, he wipes away the tears falling down my cheeks, his lips just inches from mine. "I love you. Go. Become the best damn doctor the world has ever seen. We'll always find our way back to each other."

I open my desk drawer and pull out the picture frame I've kept for the last ten years. *Why now? Why? This man isn't the man I left.* My heart breaks into a million pieces as I stare at the picture my mom took of us at the airport the day I left for college. I guess my version of forever and finding our way back to each other meant something totally different than his. Now he's a man I'd never even give the time of day to. Maybe I'll wake up tomorrow to find this was all a bad dream. I'd rather remember Mitch as the boy turning into a man, instead of the man who has turned into an asshole.

Someone knocks on my door, startling me. I drop the frame onto my stapler, shattering the glass. I sigh. If that's not a sign, I don't know what is.

One more knock before Dr. Preston Joseph sticks his head into my office. "Is everything okay, Dr. Shipman? I wanted to invite you out for drinks with me and some of the other doctors."

"Please, call me Jayna. I'm fine. I just dropped a picture frame. No big deal. And thank you. I'd love to go have drinks with everyone. That's just what the doctor ordered."

I groan inwardly. I can't believe I just said that to the very handsome doctor standing before me. Shoot me now. I can feel the blush working its way up my neck and to my cheeks.

He smiles. "Great. We're meeting downstairs by the Starbucks.

There's a really cool bar just a couple blocks up. We'll all walk, then take Ubers home...if needed."

"I'll be down in a minute. Just let me clean up my mess."

"Do you need me to help you with that?" he asks, concern evident in his voice. "I'd hate for you to cut yourself."

I wave him off. "No. It only broke into a few pieces. I can handle it, but thank you."

He shuts the door, and I look at the shards of glass on my desk. I pick up the broken frame and shake the rest of the glass into the trashcan, then pull the picture out, tossing the frame into the trash. I open my desk drawer and shove it into the back. I just can't bring myself to throw it away.

I run into the bathroom attached to my office to touch up my make-up and try to do something with my hair. It always seems to be in my face. I can never seem to remember to bring a ponytail holder with me, so I feel like I'm looking through dark curtains most of the time.

I decide to take the stairs down to avoid the possibility of being trapped on the elevator with Mitch. From now on, I'll probably come in early to hopefully avoid him all together.

A couple nurses and physicians stand around the planter in front of Starbucks, laughing and joking. They all wave me over.

"How was your first day?" asks Rebekah, one of the nurses. "We were slammed. I promise, it isn't always this crazy."

Carrington, a male nurse, chuckles. "Don't listen to her. It's usually worse."

I give them my best horrified look and start to back toward the door, then laugh.

Preston puts his hands together as if in prayer. "*Please* don't leave us." The megawatt smile he gives me makes me forget about what happened earlier today.

"Don't worry. I'd never leave you like that. I'll give you at least a week." I wink.

Preston pulls me into a hug. "Oh, thank God."

A prickling sensation starts crawling up my neck. When Preston pulls away, I look up, seeing Mitch standing in Starbucks, glaring through the glass. It makes me want to do something childish like grasp Preston's hand and pull him out the door, but I don't. Instead, I walk toward the door with Rebekah and Carrington, a bounce in my step. Preston and another physician...Stanley, I believe his name is... follow behind.

I need a drink, and fast. Ten damn years of not seeing each other, but now I can't get away from him. "How far away did you say this bar is?"

Rebekah laughs. "Just one block. A chocolatini is calling my name."

"Oh god. I love those."

I think Rebekah will be my new best friend.

CHAPTER 4

~Mitch~

If only I could convince myself I was going crazy when the smell of black currant and vanilla invaded my senses on the polluted city streets, I could forget this day ever happened. I haven't smelled that seductive scent in over ten years. That was what drew me to the woman struggling to get the box out of the back of an Uber. I nearly dropped the box when she turned. Jayna. The most beautiful woman to ever grace this earth. Her dark hair and eyes that contrast with her ivory skin. She's even more beautiful today than she was at eighteen.

I could sense the pain seeing me caused her. I know I was awful to her the last time we spoke after my mother died. We had drifted apart at that point, what with school and how demanding it was. She'd call me and fall asleep on the phone. I knew she was trying her best to keep us connected, but I'd admit, I was getting lonely with us being so far apart. I also didn't want either of us to feel like we couldn't find support from other people. Not that I thought anyone could compare to Jayna, but loneliness is sometimes hard to fight. The thought of not having her in my life tore me apart.

Then my mom got sick, and everything changed. Watching mom die, then witnessing dad fall apart broke something in me. I realized that love didn't last, and before I let that happen to me, I had to shut out the possibility.

It was the right thing for me at the time, but seeing her again, my hardened, cold heart definitely started thawing. That is something I can't risk. Love doesn't last. One way or another, your heart will be broken.

The office is buzzing this morning, everyone gathering what they need for the Monday morning meetings with the partners where we discuss our current and upcoming cases.

I don't even make it to my office before I hear my name being called. Turning, I see our secretary, Margaret, walking up.

"Mitch, Mr. Burns wants you in his office at nine thirty to discuss the Taylor case."

"Thank you, Margaret. How was your weekend. Did you and the husband have fun at the *Cats* musical?"

"We had a fantastic time. I really appreciate you getting us tickets."

"It was my pleasure. You always keep me in line, making my job so much easier."

She pinches my cheeks, just like Mom used to. "That's because you're such a thoughtful boy."

I laugh as she walks away. She wouldn't feel that way if she knew the real me.

I grab my tablet and head to Mr. Burns' office. Through his closed door, I can hear him yelling. Shit, I hope this isn't indicative of how my day is going to be.

"Just do your fucking job, Baker. We can't afford to lose another case. You best remember that if you want to stay employed here."

The door opens, and I see Baker's head hanging. "Yes, sir." He doesn't acknowledge me when he brushes past me in the hallway. You can see the embarrassment radiating off his face.

"Mitch, come in, son. It's good to see someone with ambition, because some are just lacking around here."

I smile at him. Thank God he likes me. I wouldn't want to be on his bad side. "Good morning, sir. Margaret said you wanted to meet with me."

"Yes. Mr. Taylor is coming in to meet with you this afternoon. I wanted to make sure you don't have anything else on your calendar. If you do, you need to have Margaret reschedule it. Mr. Taylor is your priority right now. Hand over any of your other cases to Brinkley and let him handle them."

"I have several new clients coming in this week. Margaret has my schedule. I plan to wrap up four cases."

"I will have her call and let those clients know Brinkley will be handling their cases." He slides a thick folder across the desk toward me. "Here is the Taylor file. It contains all the information the private investigator gathered. Unfortunately, it is very little, certainly not enough to substantiate the claims of an affair on Mrs. Taylor's part. But I have faith in you, son, and know you're the best man for the job."

"Thank you. Your confidence in me means everything. I'll take this to my office and go through it before our meeting."

His chair glides across the hardwood floor as he scoots back from his desk to stand and shake my hand. "I know you can handle this. Do me proud."

I nod and walk out the door, striding into my office.

When I drop the folder onto my desk, it opens. I about fall over when I see a picture of Mrs. Taylor. It's the woman Luke took home from the bar last night. I believe he said her name was Zee. I look at the name penned on the bottom of the picture.

Well, Mitzie Taylor, you have no idea who you are dealing with.

I smile slyly. Knowing the kinky bastard Luke is, I know he will have something I can use in this case. He never does anything without full consent from the women. I may be able to wrap this case up before it even begins.

I dial Luke's number.

"What's up, man? What has you calling this early in the day?"

"Last night, that's what."

He whistles. "Last night was off the charts for me. What about you?"

"Let's just say there's one more pissed-off female in the world. She didn't take too kindly to being brushed off."

Luke chuckles, probably shaking his head. "Did you have any projectiles thrown your way?"

"I might have, if we would've made it out of the parking lot. She was all over me, man. I'm lucky she didn't shatter the glass when I made her scream. Now, tell me about your night."

"That redhead was even kinkier than me, which is saying something. I'm going to have scratch marks on me for days. She probably paints her nails red to hide the blood when she claws the shit out of you. It hurt so good."

"Dude, that's fucked up."

"Don't knock it until you try it."

"That's okay. I'll let you keep that for yourself. I'm more about pleasure than pain."

"You know the saying. 'There's a fine line between pleasure and pain.'"

I smile. "Are you still into videoing yourself?"

"If they're down with it, then we watch it later. Makes for a *fantastic* round two."

Here goes nothing... "Did you video last night?"

Luke pauses, then snorts. "Why? You wanting to watch it or something? That's a little strange, but who am I to judge?"

I think I just threw up in my mouth a little. "Ew, no. I think Zee may be the wife of a client I'm representing in a big divorce case."

"Fuck! Are you serious? Am I going to get my ass kicked? The bitch said she wasn't married."

"No, he's done with her. In fact, he's liable to kiss you. You may be what makes this an open-and-shut case."

"Unfortunately, we didn't video ourselves last night, Mitch, but I *did* get her number. We're supposed to meet up again for another night of fun. I'm sure I can convince her to let me video it. Her bedroom had mirrors on the ceiling and one wall. She loves to watch herself."

"Damn. We need to be sure she doesn't see us together again. This case is liable to get some heavy coverage, so the sooner, the better...before my picture gets out as representing her husband in the case."

"I'll do what I can, but you'd better make sure he doesn't want to come after me for banging his wife."

"Like I said, I don't think you have anything to worry about, but I'll feel him out before I tell him about my plans."

"Okay, sounds good. I'll let you know when we plan to meet up again. Call me later and we can go grab a drink."

"You got it. Talk to ya later. And thanks, man."

After my conversation with Luke, I throw myself into work, trying to wrap up a few things before the Taylor case consumes me.

When I finally take a break and look down at my watch, I blow out a breath, seeing it's already four in the afternoon. This day is flying by. Which has kept my mind off of the woman thirty-eight floors below.

Hearing a knock on my door, I look up. "Come in."

Margaret pokes her head in, smiling. "Mr. Taylor is here to see you. Do you want to meet in here or the conference room?"

"Send him in here. Will you also bring me a fresh cup of coffee, please? I let this one get cold." I nod my head toward the Starbucks cup from this morning.

"Of course. I'll show Mr. Taylor in, then go and get you a fresh cup." Margaret leaves the office, quickly returning, gesturing Mr. Taylor into the room.

A very tall man dressed in dark jeans, boots, and white button-down shirt strides into my office. I'm man enough to admit that he is very attractive. What the hell is wrong with his wife? He has money and looks. Every woman's fantasy.

He sticks out his hand and gives mine a firm shake. "Justin Taylor. You must be Mitch Davis."

"I am indeed. It's nice to meet you. Please, have a seat. Can I offer you a drink? Coffee, water, Coke, something stronger?"

"Thank you, Mitch. Is it okay if I call you that?" At my nod, he smiles and sits. "And Margaret has already offered to get me a drink. She's picking us up a Starbucks."

"Wonderful. Let's get started then. My partners have filled me in on the basics of your case. You're not contesting the divorce, only disputing her claims of adultery and citing adultery on her part. I understand she wants half your assets. Rest assured, that isn't going to happen. I have new information that I think pretty much makes this an open-and-shut case."

"You have me intrigued, Mitch."

When I tell him about the night at the club and what I think we should do about it, a slow smile spreads across his face.

Justin sits in silence, contemplating. He opens his mouth to speak, but Margaret knocks and enters with our coffee, smiling.

After she walks out again, he takes a drink of his coffee and shakes his head. "Well, that stupid slut. I knew she wouldn't be able to keep her panties on. If he gets her on video, can we take it before the judge?"

"If she consents to videoing their time together, there is nothing she can do to stop me from using it in court. I don't think she's going to want this to go public. If I had to bet, I'd say we will have a divorce agreement in no time. Let me know what terms you are comfortable with as far as assets go. When we have the video in hand, we'll call a little meeting with her and her lawyer."

Standing, Justin reaches across my desk and offers me his hand. "I'm looking forward to working with you. I have a feeling your friend is going to be my ace in the hole. Let me know as soon as you hear anything. In the meantime, I'll think about what I'm willing to let that cheating whore have."

I walk him to the elevator. After saying our goodbyes, I smile as I turn back to my office.

Margaret grins, giving me a knowing look. "Look at that handsome smile. Do you have this one in the bag, Mitch?"

"You know I don't count my chickens before they hatch, but let's just say I'm pretty confident I'll get a settlement without having to go to court."

"I have faith in you. You're one of the best I've seen, and I've seen a lot in my old age," she laughs.

"You're not old, Margaret. You are just getting to your prime."

"Oh, stop it. You know I'm just a few years younger than dirt."

Just as I'm about to walk back into my office, Margaret's phone buzzes. She picks it up. "Yes, sir?... Yes, he's standing right here... I'll send him in." Smiling up at me, she nods at Mr. Burns' office door.

"Thanks, Margaret. Have a wonderful night. Don't stay too late."

"I have a few things to wrap up, then I'm gone."

I stride over to his door, a smile on my face, knock, and walk into his office. "You wanted to see me?"

"Well..." I give him a blank look, even though I know what he wants to hear. He rolls his eyes. "Come on. Don't leave me wondering."

I can't help but chuckle. "You doubt my abilities? You know me. This is going to be a cake walk."

His eyebrows rise. "Cake walk? What haven't you told me?"

I proceed to tell him all about Luke hooking up with Mitzie Taylor. To say he was happy is an understatement. I almost stumble forward when he slaps me on the back.

"Let's see if we can wrap up this case within a couple of weeks."

"I'm your man. It will be my top priority."

It's just after five, so I decide to leave in order to celebrate. Nothing can sour my mood...or so I thought.

I walk into Starbucks to order my last coffee of the day. As I wait,

I glance out the front window, seeing Jayna standing there with a group of people. I'm not prepared for the feelings of jealousy that run through me when another man wraps his arms around her. As Jayna pulls away from the embrace, she looks up, our eyes meeting, then she turns and walks out the door.

Knowing I'm now going to need something stronger than coffee, I call Luke and make plans to go out.

I run home and change, then schedule an Uber. Seeing that man with his arms around Jayna assured me that I'll be throwing back more than a couple drinks tonight.

CHAPTER 5

~Jayna~

I laugh when I look up at the red-lettered sign above the door of the bar. *A Really Cool Bar*.

"Wow, Preston. You weren't kidding when you said we were going to have drinks at a really cool bar."

"I never joke about unwinding." He winks.

I swallow. The last thing I need is to get involved with another doctor, no matter how handsome he is. Been there, done that. Hell, I've learned men are dogs. I'm fine by myself.

"Is everything okay?" asks Carrington, nudging me with his shoulder.

"Wonderful. I was just thinking about all the unpacking I should be doing." I smile, hoping I sound convincing.

Rebekah flings open the door, grabs my arm, and drags me in. "Chocolatinis await."

"Hell yes. Bring it."

I take in my surroundings. This is one of the coolest bars I have ever been in. There are different colored and shaped lightbulbs hanging at various levels, a welcoming glow shining around the bar. The bartop and tables are made from what looks to be recycled colored glass. I've only ever seen something like that on home remodeling shows. They are absolutely gorgeous. I make a mental note to price these when I decide to build my forever home. Pool tables and dart boards sit in the back, several games in progress, a stage to the side where they must have live music.

I'm jolted from my thoughts when Preston hands me a drink. Shit, I really was lost in my own head. I didn't even notice that we had walked to a high-top table.

He raises his glass, everyone else following. "Welcome to Texas. We are so happy to have you join the clinic."

They all cheer, and we take a sip of our drinks. This is the best chocolatini I've ever tasted. "Thanks, guys. I'm so happy to be here. You've all made this a wonderful first day."

The more Carrington drinks, the funnier he gets. When he starts to comment on people in the bar, I quickly discover he and I have the same tastes in men.

He leans into me and slurs, "I think Preston likes you. That man is H-O-T. Too bad he bats for your team."

I almost spit out my drink. "Why do you think he's into me?"

"Are you serious? He can't stop looking at you. He's practically undressing you with his eyes."

I shake my head. "You're drunk. Even if he did like me, I'm not going to date a colleague. I don't have time to date...period."

Curious, I glance over at Preston. Sure enough, he is staring right at me, which creeps me out a little. We just met.

He pats the seat next to him. "Come sit by me, Jayna. I'd like to get to know you better. Carrington and Rebekah have taken up all your attention tonight."

"That's because we are the best," Rebekah interjects, sipping her drink.

"Yes, you are *something*," I joke.

She pouts and feigns hurt, then jumps up from her seat. "I want to dance. Come dance with me, Jayna. The band just took the stage. It's country tonight. Country music is my favorite."

"I love country music, too. But I'm going to need one more drink before you'll be able to convince me to get up and dance."

Preston already stands there, handing me another drink. He leans down and whispers, "Here you go, beautiful."

Feeling slightly uncomfortable, I mumble, "Thank you."

"Let's go." Rebekah grabs my arm and pulls me to the dance floor, the band singing a Tim McGraw song.

Her enthusiasm infectious, I laugh and follow her out onto the dance floor and let go, shaking my ass with the best of them.

Watching her, I realize Rebekah can dance.

"Girl, where'd you learn to dance like that?" I ask in a raised voice to be heard over the music. "I wish I had your moves."

"If I tell you, you promise to not judge me?"

I frown. "I'd never judge."

An embarrassed blush rises up her cheeks. "I danced at a club to pay my way through nursing school."

"You're a nurse, aren't you?" I smile. "I just wish I had the confidence to dance like that."

The entire time I'm on the dance floor, I can feel Preston's gaze. I try not to let it bother me. I'm probably just overreacting.

I almost stop breathing, my heart breaking, when I glance to the side and see Mitch leaning over the back of some bleached blonde, teaching her how to shoot pool. How is it this man still has a hold on me?

Shaking my head, I turn and bump into Preston's hard chest.

"Dance with me, Dr. Shipman."

His words are more of a command than a request, but after seeing Mitch, I want to lose myself in a dance. "Okay. Just one."

Why does the next song have to be a slow one? He pulls me to him, and I almost jump away when I feel his erection pressing into me. He is oblivious to my discomfort as he sings along to "Must Be Doin' Something Right". He's not bad, but he's no Billy Currington.

When I look up, I see we are at the edge of the dance floor right next to the pool tables, and Mitch is glaring at us, anger written all over his body. His arms are crossed, feet shoulder width apart, face red. The vein in his neck throbs with each breath he takes. Well, take that, Mitchy. Go enjoy your blonde. I smirk. I shouldn't get satisfaction from his reaction, but I do.

When the song ends and a faster one starts, I'm relieved when Carrington and Rebekah pull me from Preston's arms to line dance with them. Now I feel both Preston's and Mitch's gaze on me.

As the song ends, I don't give them a chance to talk me into another dance. It's already after eleven, and I have patients coming in at eight tomorrow. I pull out my phone to order an Uber.

"Don't tell me you are calling it a night," Carrington pouts.

"I have early patients tomorrow, so yes, I'm calling it a night. I had a great time. Thank you for including me."

Rebekah hugs me. "I had so much fun. Thank you for coming."

"I'm heading out, too," Preston announces, looking at me, heat in his gaze. "Let me order us an Uber."

"That's not necessary. I've already made my request. Bye, everyone. See you in the morning."

As I walk toward the door, I feel heat on my back. I turn and see the eyes I've dreamed about looking right at me. Why does he still affect me like this after all this time? I sigh. Because I still love him. I know that will never change. I just need to convince my heart that he's not the man I fell in love with.

Preston walks up and places his hand on the small of my back, ushering me out the door. "After you, Jayna."

Relief hits me when I see my Uber waiting. My head buzzing from everything that has happened today, as well as the alcohol, I just want to go home and get into bed. Just a few more days and my life will be back home with me.

"Thank you, Preston. See you tomorrow." I don't give him time to respond as I open the door and hop into the car as quickly as I can.

CHAPTER 6

~Mitch~

The bar is packed with warm bodies and willing women. Just how I like it. I slap Luke on the back. "Country night brings out all the sexy cowgirls. I think we need to find us a couple."

We work our way up to the bar where a couple of blondes flirt with the bartender, probably trying to get free drinks. One of the girls wears a skirt so short it's borderline indecent. I elbow Luke and tilt my head.

His eyes widen. "Holy crap. I see ass cheek. She's mine."

"Go for it, man. She's all yours."

The blonde on the right wears skin-tight jeans and a low-cut blouse, but she looks more respectable. It's probably time for me to start going for classier women than usual. If... *When* I make partner, I'll be expected to bring someone with me to all the company functions.

Luke slides in between them and wraps an arm around their shoulders. "What can I get you two beautiful women to drink?"

They each turn to look at him, then me, raking their gazes up and down our bodies. You can see the appreciation all over their faces.

I wink at the girl in jeans. She ducks out from under Luke's arm and slides up next to me. "I'd love to have a Sex on the Beach," she purrs.

"Me, too," giggles blonde number one.

I signal to the bartender. "Two Coronas and two Sex on the Beach." I hand him my credit card. "Start a tab, please."

"No problem, man. Coming right up."

"Now that drinks are out of the way, how about some names?"

The girl clinging to my bicep smiles at me. "My name is Tiffany..." She nods at her friend, "and that's Susan."

"I can tell them my name," her friend pouts. "It's been my name for twenty-one years." She giggles. "I turned twenty-one yesterday. Tiffany missed my party, so we are celebrating tonight. Tiff is twenty-three. I can finally go and drink with her... Well, *legally* anyway."

Thank fuck they're legal. I was starting to worry. One thing I will not be a part of is providing alcohol to anyone underage. It's not worth losing all I've worked for.

Grabbing our drinks, we usher the women to the back and the pool tables. Luke and I have been playing since college. "Do you ladies like pool?" I ask.

"I love to play," shouts Susan, bouncing on the balls of her feet, drawing Luke's attention to her chest.

"Believe it or not, I've never played before," Tiffany admits, shrugging.

If I had a dollar for every time a woman told me that just to get me to *help* her play... They just like me leaning over them so they can grind their ass into my dick.

I smile. "Looks like tonight is your lucky night. I'll be more than happy to teach you."

"That would be great. I've always wanted to learn."

Tiffany really isn't as much of an airhead as I thought. While we wait for a pool table to open up, I've actually enjoyed talking to her. She's in her last year of the Occupational Therapy program at Texas Woman's University, so I know she isn't dumb.

I see a table open up along the back wall. Maybe it won't be as loud and we can actually have a conversation.

"Looks like a table just opened up," I tell everyone.

Luke and Susan are too busy kissing to notice. I shake my head and wad up a napkin, throwing it at his head.

He pulls back with a frown. "What the hell, man?"

"Come up for air and let's play some pool." I'm having a good time and haven't thought about Jayna once. "Do you want to play as couples or girls/guys?"

"Couples," both girls say.

"You guys would slaughter us," Susan all but whines, grating on my nerves.

Tiffany wasn't lying when she said she'd never played before. She is terrible. I stand behind her, leaning over to help her align the pool stick with the ball, when I look up and see Jayna out on the dance floor with the same man from before. He is all over her, but the look on her face shows obvious discomfort. I stand up and back away from the pool table. A low growl rumbles from my chest, ready to rip his hands off her.

"What's wrong, Mitch?" asks Tiffany, brows furrowed. She looks over to where I'm staring. "Is that your girlfriend?"

"No," I bark out. "She is an ex from years ago."

"Well, judging by your reaction, I'd say you aren't over her. If you still love her, why don't you tell her?"

"I don't believe in love. It only causes heartache."

She gives me a sad smile. "Spoken by a man who's obviously had his heart broken. I believe everyone deserves a happily ever after. It makes me sad to think you wouldn't allow yourself to have that."

"It's not for me."

Is everyone a closet psychiatrist? I swear, as soon as women find out I don't believe in love, they try and "fix" me. I'm not broken.

"This is the last thing I will say about it. Don't wait too long. You just might miss out on your future."

I laugh, trying to defuse the tension. "I thought you were going to be an occupational therapist, not a psychiatrist."

She winks and smiles. "Well, psychology plays a big role in occupational therapy. I already have a bachelor's in psychology. I'm working on getting my master's in occupational therapy."

I look up one last time and watch Jayna walk to the door. Just as she's about to leave, the same douche runs up behind her and puts his hand on her back, all but pushing her out the door. I don't know why, but I have a really bad feeling about that guy.

Susan rushes over to Tiffany, Luke trailing, a smile on his face. "Do you care if I go home with Luke? I know we came to celebrate my birthday, but...you know."

Tiffany chuckles. "Knock yourself out. Just be safe. You don't want any *unexpected* surprises keeping you from your goals." She wraps her arms around Susan.

She laughs. "Yes, Mother."

"Someone has to look out for you. Now, go. Have fun. I'll catch an Uber back to the apartment."

Susan smiles. "Don't wait up for me. You're the best."

Luke pats me on the back. "Are you okay with me leaving? You look like you and Tiffany are having a deep, meaningful conversation."

"I'm good. I'll call you tomorrow. Let's meet at the gym after work."

"Sounds good, man. See ya." He throws an arm around Tiffany's shoulders as they walk to the door.

"Looks like we both just got discarded by our wingman," Tiffany jokes.

"It sure does." I sigh. "Look, I know I've been a bit of a downer. I've really enjoyed talking to you. I'll admit. I'm an asshole. At first, I just wanted to get you into bed."

"No shit?" She laughs, rolling her eyes. "I never would have guessed that."

"But you are a great girl. I just wouldn't feel right about it. My head is all fucked up."

"I like you, Mitch. I think we could be friends." She opens her purse and pulls out a piece of paper and a pen, writing something down, then hands it to me. "Call me if you ever just want to talk. I'm a good listener. In fact, all the first-year students call me mom because I tend to mother them. That comes from being the oldest of eight. I practically raised my younger brothers and sisters."

"Eight kids? Wow. I just have one younger brother and a half-sister, who was born while I was in law school. There were times I wanted to be an only child. Henry did everything he could to drive me crazy."

"Well, eight kids isn't too far from the norm in a Catholic home. I have so many cousins I forget their names half the time."

I chuckle. "Sounds like holidays were a blast at your house."

"They still are. My youngest brother is only eight."

"My half-sister is almost five."

When Tiffany tries to stifle a yawn, I look at my watch, seeing it's already midnight. "You about to fall asleep on me?" I tease.

"I'm sorry. I've been up since five. Had to study for a test. I don't have class until nine in the morning, so I can sleep in tomorrow. I do need to head home, though."

"Let me pay for an Uber." I chuckle and pull up the app so she can enter her information, then order myself one. "It's the least I can do for all the free advice."

"Thanks so much, Mitch. I hope to run into you again. I was serious. You can always call me if you need to talk. I hope you are able to find some peace."

When my phone alerts, I look down, seeing her Uber is here. Mine is still a few minutes out. "Your ride is here. Let me walk you out."

"You're such a gentleman."

"Shh..." I glance around, as if scared somebody heard her. "I can't have people thinking I'm soft. It will ruin my image."

She chuckles as I place my hand on the small of her back and lead her through the crowd.

I can't get over how many people are still here this late on a week-night. We weave our way through the crowd outside the bar to where her ride waits at the curb.

I lean in and kiss her on the cheek. "Goodnight, Tiffany."

"Goodnight, Mitch." She climbs in and gives a little wave as the car drives off.

Not two minutes later, my ride pulls up. I look at my app, then the driver, nodding. "Are you Manny?"

"That's me. You must be Mr. Davis."

"Call me Mitch." I climb in.

"Sure thing. Traffic is crazy tonight, so it may take a little longer than usual to get home. Road construction on I-10 has two lanes closed."

"No problem. I'm not in a rush."

I settle in and unlock my phone, seeing a message from my dad that came in a few hours ago.

Hi, son. I got your message about what is going on at the business. I had plans to fly up there next week to do a site visit anyway. Thanks for giving me a heads-up. By the way, I'm so proud of you for your chance at junior partner. I know you've got it in the bag. Your mom would be proud. As soon as I book a flight, I'll give you the details.

It's late, so I don't respond. I'll text him back in the morning.

Turning off my phone, my mind wanders to Jayna. She still makes my heart race, makes me feel things I thought I wouldn't ever feel again. Feeling leaves you vulnerable, which is one thing I vowed to never be again.

CHAPTER 7

I've managed to not run into Mitch at all the rest of this week. If I'm being honest with myself, I'm actually disappointed. As much as he seems to be a womanizer, I know that isn't Mitch. He must be using that as a defense mechanism. I know I will never love another man. I gave my heart to him a long time ago, and it hasn't gotten the message that he has moved on.

One good bright spot in my week has been that Preston left for Houston yesterday to speak at a medical conference. He's coming on too strong, making me a little unsettled. I'm probably just being overly sensitive. After all, it's been over three years since I've dated anyone. I realize I wasn't in love with him, but he gave me something I love more than anything in the world. The past three and a half years have been so hard, but my world would not be the same without her. My mind drifts back to the day I told Douglas I was having his child, and how my life was changed forever.

I know Doug will be going down to the cafeteria around this time to get a cup of coffee and a bagel. He's so predictable. I meet up with him just as he walks in the doors.

He smiles when he sees me, but after a second, his smile turns into a look of concern. "You look like crap, Dr. Shipman. Are you still throwing up? You probably shouldn't have seen patients." Douglas kisses me on the cheek.

"Thanks for making a girl feel special. I'm fine to see patients. Actually, my throwing up is why I needed to talk to you." I take a deep breath. "I'm pregnant, Doug."

He grabs my arm and pulls me to the back corner of the cafeteria. "How did this happen? I thought you were on the pill. How could you be so careless?"

He might as well have punched me in the gut. I can't believe the words coming out of his mouth. I know he's rich, feels entitled, but this takes it to a whole new level. I take a deep breath to keep from screaming at him and letting the entire cafeteria know our business.

"How did I let this happen?" I whisper-shout. "I do believe it takes two to make a baby. You're a doctor, Doug. You know as well as I do that nothing is one hundred percent. You're the one who refused to use a condom. So get off your fucking high horse. Like it or not, you're going to be a father."

"I have plans for my life, Jayna. If I want my inheritance from my great-grandfather, I have to do a year with Doctors Without Borders. He was one of the original doctors who helped start it. It was a condition that I give back to others before I get it. A child is not in my plans. You need to take care of it. I'll cover the cost."

A fury I didn't know I possessed washes over me. "Go screw yourself. I'm not killing my child. Since you don't want anything to do with a baby, I will raise him or her by myself. Don't worry," I sneer. "I don't want a dime from you. All you care about is money." A sarcastic laugh breaks from me. "And to think, I thought we might actually have a future. I guess I should be thankful I see your true colors now, before I wasted more time with you."

With that, I turn and walk away. I want nothing more than to throw a cup of coffee in his face, but I have too much self-respect to make a scene.

I snap out of my memory and grab my purse. I walk up to the nurses' station to tell Rebekah and Carrington I'm leaving. "Have a good weekend. Don't party too hard."

Carrington places a hand on his hip. "Girl, you know that's impossible for me. That's what the weekends are for. The only thing that would make it better is if you were coming with us."

"My mom is bringing my little girl today, so no partying for me. Maybe once she gets settled and I can find a sitter I trust, I'll be able to go out again. The childcare in the building was one of the many reasons I was thrilled to get this job."

"And here I thought *I* was the reason," Rebekah laughs.

I smile. "Girl, you were definitely one of the main reasons."

"I can't wait to meet her. My sister is a freshman in college and has done a lot of babysitting. She worked as a nanny last summer for a family with three children. I think the youngest was two. She is always looking to make some extra money."

"That sounds wonderful. I'd love to meet her. Knowing she's your sister will definitely make it easier for me to leave Michelle with her."

"Awesome. I'll let her know. We'll set up a lunch meeting sometime soon."

"Sounds great."

I think Dallas will feel like home sooner than I expected. Honestly, the minute I laid eyes on Mitch, I felt like I was home.

* * *

When I open the door, I hear the sweetest sound in the world.

"Mommy!"

I crouch down and open my arms wide. She runs through the living room and jumps into them, making my mom laugh. Michelle places a big kiss on my cheek and starts talking.

"We rode on a big airplane. I got to eat lots of pretzels and drink juice any time I wanted. My ears went *pop, pop* when we went up, up, up into the sky."

"That was the air pressure making your ears go *pop, pop*. Did they hurt?"

"No, Mommy. Mimi gave me some gum to chew. It made it all better. Mimi knows how to make everything better."

I smile and lower her to the floor, then turn and give my mom a hug. "Hi, Mom. Thanks so much for taking such good care of my baby."

"Hi, darling. And you don't need to thank me for that. That's what Mimi's are for. She is a perfect little angel. We had so much fun. But she is excited about living in the sky. That's what she said when she saw the building. I don't know if I could get used to living in a high-rise, but this is beautiful."

"The view is beautiful at night with all the lights from downtown lighting up the skyline. I know she'll love seeing that."

"Mommy, the people and cars look so small, just like what we saw in that museum you took me to. Do you remember?"

"Of course, baby. I remember everything I do with you."

"I love my new room, Mommy. Mimi and I looked at it first. Can I go to my room and play with my dolls? I missed them so much! I only had Sally..." She holds up her favorite doll, "and she missed her friends, too." She heads toward her room.

"Have fun, sweetheart. If you need me, I'll be right here in the living room with Mimi."

"Okay, Mommy."

I smile. "Do you want some coffee, Mom? It won't take me but a second to pop a pod into the Keurig."

"No, thank you. I had a cup when I got here. I hope you don't mind."

"Don't be silly. You are welcome to anything in my home.

"So..." I swallow. "You're never going to believe who I ran into outside my office building on my first day of work."

My mom furrows her brow. "Who? Do I even want to know? Please tell me it wasn't Doug the douche."

I laugh. "*Mom!* Did you really just call Doug a douche?"

"Yes, I did. If the shoe fits..."

"I haven't heard from Doug since the day Michelle was born and he told me to not list him on the birth certificate. I don't even know why I called him in Africa. He's back in the United States now and has a practice in San Francisco. That is the last thing I heard from one of our mutual friends, who also did Doctors Without Borders. He has no idea Michelle is actually Doug's. I plan on keeping it that way."

"What a relief. I never liked him."

I snort. "You never liked *anyone* after Mitch."

"You've got that right. He was one special boy." Her face falls. "You know, your father and I always felt like we were the reason you two didn't work out. We just wanted you both to get your education, thinking you would find your way back to each other. I regret, more than you'll ever know, that I didn't tell you about his mother being sick. I did what I thought was best."

I place my hand on her arm. "I know, Mom. What if I told you that the person I ran into on my first day *was* Mitch?"

Mom's jaw drops open. "Are you serious? He's here? I figured he was still in Arkansas with his family."

"Me, too. I was struggling to get my stuff out of the Uber. Imagine my surprise when a man asked if I needed help and it was Mitch! It took everything I had to not faint."

"Wow, Jayna. What did he do?"

"He looked just as surprised as me, then bought me a coffee at the Starbucks in my building. *Oh,* that's another thing. His office is in the *same* building."

She sucks in a breath. "Are you kidding me?"

"I wish I were. But he's not the same Mitch I knew ten years ago."

"What do you mean?"

"Well, he has this...hardness about him. I saw glimpses of the old

Mitch, but that didn't last long. Almost like he realized it and put on the mask again. When I excused myself to use the bathroom so I could calm my racing heart, I came back out to see him having an intense conversation with some woman. He was awful to her, Mom, then told me he just uses women. It made me sick."

"That doesn't sound like Mitch at all." A look of guilt and sadness quickly passes over her face. "I feel like this is all my fault. If I hadn't kept Emily's diagnosis from you, then told you when she died, maybe you two would be together now. I know he was very angry and bitter that you didn't call him. He must hate me."

"I honestly don't know. All I *do* know is he's not the same. I have successfully avoided him this week because seeing him is painful, yet not seeing him is painful, too. I keep replaying the words he said to me before I left for college. '*I love you. Go. Become the best damn doctor the world has ever seen. We'll always find our way back to each other.*'"

My chin starts to tremble. "Do you think this is a sign? Is this us finding our way back to each other? As much as I've tried to forget him over the years, I just can't, Mom. I still love him." I wipe away the tear trickling down my cheek.

Mom pulls me into a hug, my tears starting to fall freely.

After a few minutes, I take a deep breath and pull away, wiping my eyes. "Thanks, Mom. I feel better already."

"You'd better wash your face before Michelle comes out and sees you like this. She's smart and will know you're upset."

"You're right. I'll be back in a minute. Think about what you want for dinner."

When I pass Michelle's room, I stop on the other side of her door and listen to her talking to her dolls.

"Sally, give Mary Beth a hug. We haven't seen her in a week. Mary Beth, ask Sally if she likes our house in the sky. I love it, and that's all that matters." She goes back and forth with the dolls, telling each one what to say.

I chuckle and head to the bathroom.

After washing up, I feel one hundred times better. When I reach Michelle's room, I poke my head in. "What would you like for dinner, sweetie pie?"

"Pizza!" she yells.

She is her mother's daughter. Pizza is my favorite, too. Mitch and I ate pizza at Pop's Pizza Company every Friday night. "Pizza it is. Do you want to go get it or have it delivered?"

"Um..." She looks around her room, smiling slightly. "Delivered, please."

"You got it. I'll let you know when it gets here."

An hour later, we are all curled up on the couch eating pizza and watching *Cinderella*. Mom keeps looking at me with concern, almost like she thinks I'm going to fall apart again. As I've sat here, contemplating the last week, I've decided I'm not going to let my past get in the way of my future. If Mitch is happy the way he is, I'm in no position to judge. Maybe he'll eventually see that what he's doing is not who he is.

CHAPTER 8

~Mitch~

It's been a productive week, in spite of my mind wandering to Jayna more often than I want it to. Mr. Taylor and I worked out a divorce settlement. Mitzie is lucky her soon-to-be ex agreed to give her anything. She's contributed nothing to their marriage, and from all the research I've done, is quite the spender.

I gather up my stuff and walk out of my office, seeing Margaret still sitting at her desk. "Go home, Margaret. Why are you still here?"

"Just making sure I have all the files ready for Brinkley."

I shake my head. "You're the best. I don't know what I'd do without you. I don't think he will need to take too many more. I'm hoping to have the Taylor case wrapped up soon."

Her brows raise in question. "You must have something up your sleeve. I have a feeling Mrs. Taylor isn't going to know what hit her."

"Just doing my job. Have a wonderful weekend. Tell the mister I said hello."

Margaret smiles. "You do know calling him that gives him a big head, right? We both know who's the boss in our house.

Try not to work all weekend, Mitch. I think it's time for you to start looking for a young lady, and you can't do that if you're working all the time."

I snort. "Don't hold your breath. That won't happen any time soon."

"It always happens when we least expect it."

I'm still shaking my head when the elevator doors close. As the car stops on the second floor, I hold my breath, not sure whether or not I want it to be Jayna getting on. It's almost seven. She has to be gone for the day. When the doors open, I admit, I'm disappointed when it's the cleaning lady.

I step off the elevator on the ground floor and glance into the Starbucks to see if Jayna is in there. No luck.

Ten years... Why did she have to show up here after ten years?

I make my way to the parking garage and climb into my car. My phone starts to ring as I pull out. Seeing Luke's name, I press the hands-free button.

"Hey, man. What's up?"

"Mitch... I know we talked about hitting the bar tonight, but I don't think you'll mind me backing out when you hear why."

"If it includes Mitzie Taylor, I don't mind one bit. Besides, it's been a long week. A night at home with a beer and TV sounds good to me."

"Good. So, I have plans with Mitzie at my place. The video recorder is already set up. She seemed excited when I told her I like to video myself having sex. I think I can have what you need by tomorrow."

"I love you, man," I chuckle. "If you pull this off, I will owe you *big time*. To cover our asses, make sure you have her saying she agrees to being taped before you do anything. I want this to be airtight."

"Trust me, man. This isn't my first rodeo. I always make them sign a consent form. I don't want to be sued later. I'll have it in writing."

I snort. "You are one kinky mother, and I couldn't be happier. Have fun, just be sure to wrap it up. There's no telling how many men she's been with."

"Tight as a drum, man. Talk to you tomorrow."

Laughing, I end the call and drive home with a smile on my face. Things are starting to fall into place. I never dreamed, at twenty-eight, I'd be this close to making junior partner.

I'm starving, so when I stop at a red light, I call and order a pizza, smirking when I remember Jayna. Friday's are for pizza. Too bad Dallas doesn't have a Pop's Pizza Company. Thinking about it brings back both happy and sad memories. All the times Jayna and I went there were full of fun and laughter. We were at Pop's the first time I told her I loved her and leaned in to suck some red sauce off her bottom lip. The last time I ate pizza from Pop's was just before I received the news my mother was dying. It's time for me to associate pizza with happy times again.

When I get home, the doorman smiles and opens the door. "Good evening, Mr. Davis."

"Hello, Mac. How's your day been?"

"My day's been great. Thanks for asking."

"I have some pizza being delivered. Just send them up when they get here. You're welcome to help yourself to a slice. It will be our secret." I wink.

"Now, you know I can't eat your pizza. I'll get fired. Besides, my waistline doesn't need it." He chuckles and pats his stomach.

"You can always hit the gym with me," I say as I walk into the elevator.

He shakes his head. "I'll leave that to you young'uns. I'm too old."

I let myself into the apartment and kick off my shoes before I grab a beer from the fridge and turn on ESPN. In no time at all, the door-bell rings with the arrival of my dinner.

After drinking more than a few beers and eating more than half of a large pizza, I'm feeling sentimental, which is why I'm staring at a picture I've had in a box in my closet ever since I moved to Dallas. It's the picture Jayna's mother took of us on the day she left for Harvard. There was a mixture of happiness for the future and sadness at having to leave each other. She looked breathtakingly beautiful, but nothing compares to how beautiful she looks now.

My phone buzzing on the coffee table startles me awake. The sun shines through the glass doors to my terrace. How the hell did I sleep on the couch all night?

I sit up and hear something fall to the floor. Looking down, I see the picture of me and Jayna. I don't know how it didn't shatter. A sign maybe?

I pick up my phone and see it's my dad. I rub a hand over my face as I answer. "Hi, Dad."

"Hi, son. I just booked my flight. I'll be landing Tuesday at eight thirty in the morning."

"Shit. I have a nine o'clock meeting. I can try and reschedule it."

"Don't worry about it, son. I had planned on getting a rental. I need to be able to pop in and out of the gym and don't want you to have to worry about rearranging your schedule for me. I just wanted to let you know what time I'd be in town."

"My meeting shouldn't last too long. Why don't you come back to my place, drop your stuff off, then meet me at the office. We can get a coffee before you go to the gym."

"That sounds good. I'll see you on Tuesday. Love you."

"I love you, too, Dad."

After I hang up, I pick up the picture and put it back into the box. Nothing good can come of the *what ifs*. I'm perfectly happy with my life.

I look at my watch and see it's nine thirty. Luke won't be up for another hour or more, depending on how much he drank and how late he was up. I decide to throw on some shorts and head out for a run.

I take an Uber to Trammell Crow Park. I love it here. The trails are amazing, the skyline backdrop beautiful. I pop in my earbuds and take off at a jog, ready for a relaxing run. It seems the universe, however, has other plans. Every song makes me think of Jayna. Maybe if she hadn't shown up in Dallas a week ago, I wouldn't be thinking about her. Yeah, that's a lie. Once that bartender called me *Mitchy*, I started thinking about her.

I run faster, my heart pounding in my chest. I feel a tingling in my neck and look around. I see kids running and playing. A few people sit at picnic tables. My gaze zeros in on a woman with dark, curly hair sitting in the grass, her back to me. If I didn't know better, I'd think it was Jayna. Until I see a small child with the same black curls running around her with a doll in her hands. I shake my head.

I keep running to try and put all things Jayna out of my mind.

Twenty minutes later, my phone rings, Luke's name popping up on the screen. I slow my pace to a jog and answer. "Tell me what I want to hear, my man," I pant.

"Are you running? God, I hope you didn't answer during sex."

"Very funny, asshole. Yes, I'm running. That's why I have a better body than you do."

"If you're going to be a dick, I'll just hang up and not tell you that I have video footage of one of the hottest nights of my life."

I chuckle. "I take back what I said."

"I have her recorded consent, as well as signed consent. She was even dumb enough to sign it with her last name. She did sign it Zee, but everyone will know she is one in the same."

"You're a freaking genius, Luke. I owe you."

"You'd better believe it. The only thing I regret is that she will hate me after this. I wasn't kidding when I said the sex was hot. You'd better be on the lookout for someone even better."

"Dude, I think you do a good job on your own. It's like you have a sixth sense in finding kinky women."

He snickers. "I do seem to have a built-in radar."

"I should have known when I found those erotic romance books at your house."

"I told you, those belonged to my sister. I won't lie and say I didn't read them to see what all the hype was about, though."

"You can read whatever the hell you want. When can we meet up? I have a meeting with my boss on Tuesday at nine. This will make his day."

"How about Sunday? Let me have one more night with Zee before it all blows up. Maybe I can get you even more dirt."

"Sunday is great. Enjoy." I hang up, shaking my head with a smile on my face. Life is good.

CHAPTER 9

~Jayna~

We arrive at the airport with time to spare, so I pull into the short-term parking so we can take a few minutes to say our goodbyes. Mom and I climb out of the car and go to the back seat to retrieve her luggage and unbuckle Michelle from her car seat. Michelle squirms, trying to get the buckles unfastened by herself.

"Michelle," I scold, "what have I told you about trying to get out of your car seat by yourself?"

"I'm sorry, Mommy. I was just ready to get out."

"It's okay, sweetheart. Just don't do it again. It's not safe."

She nods her little head, looking down. "Yes, ma'am."

I look over to Mom, who is trying to mask her sadness with a smile. "I hate that you have to go home already, but I know Dad misses you."

"You know he can't make it more than a day or two without me taking care of him," she jokes. But it's true. Now that they're retired, they do everything together.

Michelle, tears running down her cheeks, throws her arms around Mom's waist. "I'm going to miss you, Mimi. You and Pop have to come back to see me and Mommy."

Mom kneels in front of her. "My sweet little princess, we will be here to see you next month. You be a big girl and help your mommy get settled in your house in the sky."

She smiles. "Okay, Mimi. I'll be a big girl. I will miss you."

Mom gives her a big squeeze and a kiss on the tip of her nose, then stands and pulls me into a hug. "I love you, sweetie. I'm just a phone call away if you need me. Don't let seeing Mitch bring you down. Maybe this is fate. Unfortunately, he's a man, which means it'll take him longer to figure that out."

"Don't hold your breath, Mom. I'll be fine. Michelle is all I need. Have a safe flight home. Call me as soon as you land. Give Daddy a big hug and kiss from me."

"I will, honey." She turns and gives Michelle one last hug before grabbing her bag and walking through security, turning one last time to wave.

I grasp Michelle's hand and squeeze. "Who wants to go to the park for a picnic?"

Her eyes light up as she starts jumping up and down. "Me! I want to go to the park. Do they have swings?"

"I'm sure they do. I packed your favorite. PB&J and Kettle potato chips. Let's not forget the brownies for dessert."

"You're the bestest, Mommy."

The other day, Carrington told me about Trammell Crow Park. He said his nieces and nephews love going there when they come to visit. I pull up Google maps so I can find my way there from the airport.

For a Saturday, the traffic is crazy. It took us longer to get to the park than it should have. Once I park, I unbuckle Michelle and grab our stuff, then lead her to an open spot, spreading out the blanket.

A weird feeling, like a zap of electricity, passes through me as I sit there, watching Michelle dance around with one of her dolls. I could swear I sense Mitch, but that's crazy.

I turn and see a man running on the trail that circles the park. My breath catches in my throat. I think that *is* Mitch. Watching him for a few minutes, I blow out a breath when he doesn't see us. If he did, he would have come over. Curiosity always did get the better of him.

We spend a few hours at the park, Michelle making several friends. One mom, Bonnie, told me about a play group that meets one weekend a month and goes to different child-friendly locations around the area. It sounds like fun, and she seems like a good friend to have. Bonnie's husband is a dentist whose office is only a block down from mine. She said she frequently walks to the Starbucks in my building when she's helping out at his clinic. We exchanged numbers, agreeing to meet for coffee during my break Tuesday morning.

Michelle doesn't want to leave the park, but I'm tired and ready to go. Once she sees me packing up our stuff, she starts yawning and rubbing her eyes, all the fight leaving her.

By the time we get home, Michelle is fast asleep in the back seat of the car. All that fresh air and running around wore her out. That park is like an oasis in the middle of all the hustle and bustle. I make a mental note to take Michelle there one evening. I'm sure the lights from the city are beautiful.

I gently scoop her up and carry her toward the building. It's only two o'clock, so I figure she can sleep another hour and still go to bed at a normal time tonight. The doorman sees me coming and quickly opens the door, smiling down at Michelle, then pushes the elevator button for me.

* * *

Michelle was so excited to be starting her new *school*, as she called it.

She walked in and announced that her name was Michelle Shipman and I was Dr. Shipman, but she just called me Mommy.

I don't know why, but I still can't get used to being called doctor. My parents tell me all the time to be proud of what I've accomplished and enjoy being called Dr. Shipman. Michelle has grown up hearing them say this, so I guess that's why she introduced me that way.

I'm proud of myself because, during the day, I only called down to the daycare one time to check on her. They went on and on about how good she was doing. I knew she would do fine. *I'm* the one having the trouble.

Dr. Joseph found every opportunity he could to talk to me today. I could have sworn I even saw him taking a picture of me on his phone. If that were true, it would be just too creepy.

Once my last patient walks out of the room at four forty-five, I rush back to my office to grab my stuff because I need to pick up Michelle by five. However, Preston is waiting as I come out of my office.

I give him a smile and try to skirt around him, but he grabs my arm. "Let me walk you out."

"I really have to run. My daughter is waiting for me to pick her up. I'll see you tomorrow, Preston."

He almost looks angry, but he quickly schools his features and nods. "See you tomorrow, Jayna."

Not wanting to get on the elevator, just in case he follows me, I run down the stairs. I'm weirded out by Preston's behavior. It's almost stalkerish and beginning to make me feel uncomfortable.

Michelle is all smiles when I pick her up. She couldn't wait to tell me all about her day as I buckle her into the car.

"Mommy, I have a new friend named Harry. He is three. I'm in the three-year-old room, even though I'm only two. I get to be with the big kids."

"You're *almost* three."

"I know, Mommy, but the other kids are all already three. My teacher told me I'm so smart."

"You are. Mommy is so proud of you. You ready to go home?"

"Yes, but can we stop at Chick-Fil-A for dinner? I want some nuggets and mac and cheese. Please.

"You know I can't say no to Chick-Fil-A. Let's go eat some chicken, you little nugget."

She laughs. "I'm not a nugget, Mommy."

"You're not?" I narrow my eyes in the rearview mirror. "I thought you were my little nugget."

"I'm your *big girl*."

"That's right. You are such a big girl. If you eat all your nuggets, you can play in the play area for a little bit."

She ate every bite, then played until exhausted, her eyes drooping on the drive home.

Once there, Michelle is barely able to stay awake for her bath. I think her first day at daycare and playing afterward wore her out. She's sound asleep before her head hits the pillow. Now it's my turn to take a long bath and have a glass of wine.

I fill the tub and turn on the jets, then lay back and close my eyes. This reminds me of the hot tub that night all those years ago. I can't reconcile the Mitch of today with the Mitch from then.

"Mitch, come out onto the balcony. Is that a hot tub?"

"I told you we could just relax in the hot tub if you weren't ready for more."

"I want to do both," I say, pulling my shirt over my head. I hear a sharp intake of breath as my bra hits the floor and I start to shimmy out of my shorts and panties.

When Mitch strips out of his jeans and t-shirt, my heart starts racing. Our lives are about to change. The bond between us will be stronger than ever.

The ringing of my phone startles me from my thoughts. Who could be calling me at nine o'clock at night? It's a local number, but not one I recognize. I let it go to voicemail.

When I get a notification, I check it. My eyes widen when I hear Preston's voice.

"*Hi, Jay... Is it okay for me to call you Jay? I was sitting here thinking about you. I hope your daughter had a good first day. Maybe I can take you both out for dinner sometime. I'd really like to get to know you better. I'll see you in the morning, beautiful. Sweet dreams.*"

Chills crawl all over me, making me shiver. There is something... off about him. I've got to be overreacting. If he was dangerous, surely Rebekah or Carrington would've said something, right? Hell, Carrington practically drooled over him at the club. Maybe I'm just imagining things. Maybe I can ask the other women in the office without being obvious.

CHAPTER 10

~Jayna~

After tossing and turning most of the night, thinking about Mitch, I'm in desperate need of my coffee this morning. It was all I could do to not get a cup first thing, but I was running late after dropping Michelle off at daycare. I barely made it in time for my first appointment at eight.

Luckily, my first several appointments fly by. I look at my watch to see it's almost ten. I don't have another patient until eleven, so I send Bonnie a quick text to let her know I have a break.

She responds immediately, telling me she's on her way. I grab my purse and stop at the receptionist's desk.

"Mary, I'm meeting a friend for a bit. If you need me, just text. I'll be back before eleven."

"No problem, Dr. Shipman."

I smile. "Please, call me Jayna. No need to be so formal."

"I'll try. Most doctors insist on being addressed as such."

"Well, I'm not most doctors." I wave and head down the stairs, walking toward Starbucks.

It's not crowded this time of the morning, so I find a table without difficulty, deciding to wait to order until Bonnie gets here. As I watch people coming and going, I hear the barista say, "Benson."

I sit up straight, not moving. Can it be? Slowly, I turn around in my seat just as Benson, Mitch's dad, turns from the counter, stopping abruptly.

"Jayna?" Tears form in my eyes when I stand. He holds his arms out. "Come here, sweet girl." I almost run into his embrace. "It's been too long since I've seen you. How are you, sweetheart?"

"Benson, I'm so sorry about Emily," I sob. "You must hate me for not being there for you."

He pushes me away and holds me at arm's length. "I could never hate you, honey. You're like a daughter to me. I understand. Your parents told me they kept Em's cancer diagnosis from you. They were only doing what they thought was best. I'm sorry for how Mitch treated you. He was trying to hold it together for me, but was falling apart on the inside. He took it out on you."

"I deserved all he gave me."

Feeling my phone buzz in my pocket, I wipe my face and pull it out, seeing a text from Bonnie.

I'm sorry to do this, but the receptionist's daughter is sick and she has to pick her up from school. I have to cover for her. I hope we can meet soon. Again, I'm so sorry.

I type out a quick reply.

No worries. We'll meet up another time. Have a good day.

"Bad news?" Benson asks, seeing my furrowed brows.

"Not at all. I was supposed to meet a friend here, but she isn't able to make it."

He smiles. "Well, this is my lucky day then. Can I buy you a coffee?" He points at me. "Skinny mocha, right?"

I laugh. "I can't believe you remember. Yes, I'm addicted, but you don't have to buy me a coffee."

"Nonsense. I'll be right back. I want to hear all about what's happened over the past ten years. I can't believe it's been so long. It doesn't seem possible."

"Thank you, Benson."

My head a swirl of memories, I hope I can get out of here before Mitch walks in. That would be too much for my aching heart to take. Seeing Benson has made me acutely aware of how much I have missed over the years.

"Here you go, sweet girl. One skinny mocha with an extra shot of espresso."

I take the cup, gesturing for Benson to sit down at my table. "Thank you. I need it more right now than you know. I didn't get much sleep last night, so I was running late this morning and missed my first cup."

"That just won't do. Emily was a bear if she didn't get a cup." He smiles.

I take a sip of my coffee, then set down the cup. "So, tell me about your daughter. I want to know all about little Emily."

Giving me the most heartwarming smile I've ever seen, he shakes his head. "She is the most amazing little girl. So much like her name-sake. I swear, there has to be a supernatural connection between the two of them. The boys absolutely adore her, and vice versa. Marley is a wonderful mother, as I knew she would be."

He takes a sip of his coffee, then sets the cup down, blowing out a breath. "Is it weird that I fell in love with Em's best friend?"

"Not at all. Emily loved you both. I know she's happy that you found joy with each other."

"She had it all planned out, you know. Em was sneaky that way. As soon as she found out she was terminal, she had it in her mind that I would find love again. She insisted Marley wanted to be there for her, so Emily demanded she be the one to take care of her, not some hospice nurse.

"After she died, Marley and I became really close, then we found letters basically saying that Em wanted us to be together."

I can't stop the tears when I see Benson's eyes pooling with his own. "That is so beautiful. She loved you like no other. You two were such an inspiration to Mitch and me. I just wish we could have been as dedicated to each other as you both were."

"Oh, sweet girl, don't give up hope. Sometimes things don't work out on our timetable, but it will eventually. I didn't think I would ever love anyone other than Em, but fate had other plans. Marley will never replace her, but I love her just as much."

I sigh. "I still love him, you know. Believe me, I tried to forget about him. I even thought I might have found love again. I was wrong.

"But Mitch has changed, Benson. He's not the same man I knew all those years ago. I've seen how he treats women and, to be quite honest, it disgusts me."

He places a hand on my arm. "I'm not making excuses for him, but like I said, he fell apart after his mom died. It wasn't until after I was able to heal myself that I saw the depths of his pain. Seeing me hit rock bottom affected him tremendously. I think that's why he treats women like he does. He lives by the old saying, 'Hurt them before they hurt you.'

"I *know* he still loves you, Jayna. If you truly still love him, give him some time to see that he is capable of love and allow him to open his heart again. He's still a good man. Hang on to the Mitch that you remember."

"I want to. It's just that so much has changed."

The timer on my phone chimes, telling me my break is over. "I'm sorry, Benson. I need to head back up for my next appointment. It was so good to see you. How long will you be in town?" We both stand.

"I'll be here a few days. I need to check in on the gym. Mitch told me some things he's seen, so I want to see for myself and get it fixed. Maybe we can get together for dinner one night before I fly back to Fayetteville."

"That sounds great. Here." I hand him my phone. "Enter your number. I'll text you so you have mine."

He takes it and types. "Done. Love you, sweet girl." He pulls me into a fatherly hug.

When I hear somebody clear their throat behind me, I pull away and turn, sucking in a breath as I stare into familiar green eyes.

"Jayna, Dad... I didn't expect to see you two together."

Benson pulls Mitch into a warm embrace. "Hi, son. Imagine my surprise when I ran into Jayna. It was almost like it was meant to be." He looks at me and winks. I stifle a groan. I have a feeling Benson is going to be playing matchmaker while in town.

"I really need to head back to the office. It was so good to see you, Benson. Bye, Mitch." I almost run out the door.

CHAPTER 11

~Mitch~

My heart skipped a beat when I walked into Starbucks and saw Jayna in my father's arms. It transported me back to better times. My parents and Jayna were as close as could be. They thought of her as their daughter. I know it was hard on them when we left for college, because it was like they had to say goodbye to two children.

I watch her all but run out the door, then turn back to my dad. "Well, that was unexpected." I take the seat Jayna vacated.

"I've missed her, son. It was like seeing a family member. I know it can't be easy on you, though."

"It's fine. I don't do love anymore. We were just kids anyway."

"Listen to yourself, Mitch. This is your *father* you're talking to. That's a load of bullshit, and you know it. I never dreamed it would take you so long to realize how much time you've wasted being scared and angry."

"Keep telling yourself that, Dad, but this is me. I'm fine just the way I am."

"She still loves you, you know. I can see it in her eyes. It's not every day you find your soulmate at such a young age, but you did. I just wish you weren't so stubborn and would realize that. She won't wait forever. If you're not going to swallow your pride, someone will come along and snatch her up."

I wave a hand through the air. "I don't want to talk about this anymore. Have you been to the gym yet? I thought you might change your mind and decide to go there first."

My dad studies me for a moment, then shakes his head. "No. I came straight here after dropping my bags off at your place. I'm glad I did, too, or I might not have run into Jayna."

"Well, Mr. Fate, you probably would've run into her at some point."

"So, how did your meeting go?"

"It went great." I smile. "I have video footage of my client's cheating wife. She would be crazy not to settle for what my client is offering. In my opinion, he's being too generous, but he just wants it over with as little publicity as possible. To say my boss is thrilled is an understatement. He told me if the case is settled without going to court, I'll have the papers on my desk Monday morning making me junior partner."

"That's wonderful, son. I'm so proud of you. I know your mother is smiling down on you right now." He gets a twinkle in his eye. One I know means he's up to something. "The only thing that would make your mom even more proud would be for you to pull your head out of your ass and open up your heart. Do you think it's just a coincidence that Jayna's back in your life after all these years?"

I snort. "Let's just agree to disagree. Do you want me to come with you to the gym? I have time."

"I'd love you to come with me, but you drive." Dad tosses me the keys to his rental. "I hate driving in Dallas."

I roll my eyes when I look at the keys. "A Tesla, Dad? Really? I can't believe you rented a Tesla. I'd be happy to drive my car, but this might be fun."

He shrugs. "I wanted to see what all the hype is about. Actually, this Tesla Model S is quite nice. I may have to give in and buy Marley one."

We leave the hustle and bustle of the office building to fight the madness on the streets, the car parked right out front. "How'd you manage to get such a good spot this time of day?"

"Lucky, I guess. Someone was pulling out right as I got here."

I unlock the doors and we climb in. Time to see what this car can do.

I pull out and gun it a little, the car responding immediately. I can't believe how much power this thing has. But it's not my baby. I wouldn't trade my car for anything. "I think you should surprise Marley with one of these. It's very nice."

"I just might do that for her birthday. I'll decide after driving this one for a few days."

I zip in and out of traffic. In no time at all, we park at the gym. When Dad walks through the doors, I can see the surprise on his employees' faces.

"Uh... Mr. Davis. What a surprise. I didn't know you were coming today." Neal, the manager, seems nervous. He should be, because he hasn't been running this gym the way he should be. He is too chummy with the employees and members. Friendly is good, but he's way too lax.

Dad holds out his hand, the two shaking. "I was in town visiting my son and wanted to check in and see how things were going. I have some concerns. I hear there is a lot of hanging out on the equipment, blocking members from using them. I understand people like to socialize, but it's your job to make sure the machines aren't being held up. Please remind the workers that part of their job is to circulate and encourage people to be courteous and step away when they are talking or on their phones."

Neal fumbles over his words. "Yes... Yes, sir. I-I will be on top of it. The employees are just afraid of a member getting upset if they say something."

"Tell them to give the members my personal number if they have a problem and I'll be happy to talk to them. I've been wanting to try something out, and I think now is a good time. I'm going to get small lockers and put them behind the desk. Any member who checks in their phone will be eligible to win a free month. They can still have their phones if they want to listen to music, but this should cut down on the people just sitting on the equipment and checking their social media."

"That sounds like a great idea, Mr. Davis." Neal glances at me, knowing I had to be the one who'd said something to him. Tough shit. He needs to step it up and do a better job.

Dad nods. "I'm glad you think so.

"Next thing... I'd like to meet as many of the employees as possible this week so they can put a face with a name. I'll be happy to address any questions or concerns they may have. I will be in and out for the rest of the week."

"I look forward to having you here. I'm sure everyone else will feel the same way."

"Mitch and I are going to lunch. I'll see you later this evening."

"See you soon."

As soon as we're out the door, I elbow Dad in the side. "I think you intimidated the shit out of him, Dad. I've never seen him look so nervous."

"That just tells me he knows he's not doing his job to the best of his ability. That shit will stop today, or he will be looking for a new job. I need a manager who is on top of things. If you are bothered by something, Mitch, there's a good chance other members are, too. I need to try and blend in to feel out some of the members and get their opinions."

"It is crazy busy between four and seven. That's when it's nearly impossible to get on the machines. Like I said, it's usually because people are chatting and taking up space.

"Let's grab some lunch, then I need to get back to the office."
"Sounds good. What's good to eat around here?"
"Meso Maya is my favorite Mexican restaurant."
"Mexican sounds good to me."

CHAPTER 12

~Jayna~

I rush up to the office and through the back entrance. I buzz Mary to let her know I'm back.

"Thanks for letting me know. Your eleven o'clock just called and canceled. They were caught up in a meeting and will have to reschedule. I'll let you know when your eleven twenty gets here."

"Thanks, Mary."

I have to admit that I'm a bit relieved my eleven o'clock canceled. My brain is still spinning after the unexpected surprise at Starbucks. It was wonderful seeing Benson. He treated me just like he always did, which brought tears to my eyes. I've missed him and Emily so much. It hurts me knowing that I'll never see her again. I still can't believe she's gone. Seeing him also reinforced that I'm not over Mitch, not by a long shot, even with him acting like he does. Could Benson be right? Will *my* Mitch eventually come back to me, or is that just a silly dream?

A quick knock sounds on my door. Before I can tell whomever it is to come in, it opens. Who the hell just opens a door without being told it's okay to come in?

"Where have you been?" Preston asks. "I've been looking all over for you."

Taken aback, I blink at him. "I was getting a coffee at Starbucks."

"You really should let me know if you're going to be out of the office."

I close my eyes, taking a deep breath to calm myself. He's really starting to piss me off. Who the hell does he think he is? "I let Mary know," I grit out.

"I was just worried something might have happened to your daughter or something. I don't mean to overstep."

The hell you don't, I think to myself, barely managing to not voice my thoughts out loud. "It's fine. Now, if you'll excuse me, I have some stuff to finish up before my next patient gets here."

"I will let you get back to it, but first, tell me you will have lunch with me today."

"I'm sorry, but I can't. My next break isn't until two. I brought something to eat in between patients."

"One day, you're going to give in and let me take you out." He winks and walks out the door.

I roll my eyes. Dream on, buddy.

Thank goodness we are non-stop patients for the rest of the day. My eleven twenty arrived early, which helped since we had several emergency patients to work in. When I finally get a break, I check my phone, seeing a text from Benson.

It was so good seeing you today. If you don't already have plans, I'd love for you to have dinner with me and Mitch tomorrow night. I hope to hear from you soon.

I smile and quickly respond.

It was great seeing you, too. I would love to have dinner with you, but I'll have to get back to you later tonight to let you know for sure. I doubt Mitch will be happy to find out you've made plans with me.

Benson responds almost immediately.

No worries. Leave Mitch to me. I look forward to hearing from you.

I lock the screen on my phone, then slide it back into my pocket and go to find Rebekah. Looks like I'll be needing her sister's babysitting services sooner than I thought. I see her sitting at the nurses' station.

"Hey, Bek. Do you think your sister would be available tomorrow night to watch Michelle for a few hours?"

She raises her eyebrows. "Do you have a hot date already?" She leans closer and lowers her voice. "Did you finally give in to Preston? He's been trying to get me to talk you into going out with him, but I told him I wasn't getting in the middle of an office romance."

I growl. "First off, it's not a hot date, and secondly, I'm *never* going to date Preston. I ran into the father of an old friend this morning. He asked me to join him for dinner tomorrow night."

"Well, crap. I was hoping you'd picked up a hottie." She laughs.

"I didn't say he wasn't hot, he's what women would call a silver fox, but he's like a dad to me."

Her eyebrows shoot up. "I like older men. Is he single?"

"No." I smile. "He's very happily married."

"Damn." She waves her hand through the air. "I will talk to my sister and let you know what she says."

"Thanks. You're the best."

"Don't thank me yet. Let's hope she's available."

"No worries. If she can't do it, it's fine."

"By the way, Mary just buzzed back to say your four o'clock is here. I was just about to get him checked in."

"Okay. I'm going to take a quick bathroom break first."

* * *

After Mr. Norris walks out the door, I sigh. He is such a sweet old man, but he is lonely...and perfectly healthy. He just wanted someone to talk to. After telling me about a constipation issue he thought he had, he told me his life story while I examined him. His abdomen wasn't tender, and I felt no blockage, so I gave him some samples of a laxative, instructed him to take it daily, and to return if he was still having concerns.

I rush out the door, quickly waving to Carrington and Mary, then stop at the elevator, pushing the button.

I'm checking my email on my phone when the elevator doors open, not paying attention to what I'm doing. As I step forward, I almost run directly into Mitch, my eyes widening. Those eyes. That body. It makes it almost impossible to tear my gaze away.

"Mitch," I whisper.

"Hello, Jayna. You sure made my dad's day today. He has missed you, you know."

I smile shyly as I step on. "I've missed him, too."

What am I going to do? Once we reach the first floor, Mitch is going to see me walk down the hallway toward the daycare. I glance down at my watch and see it's only a few minutes before five. No chance of delaying.

The elevator quickly reaches the first floor. The lobby is filled with people, making me hopeful I can get lost in the crowd.

"Mommy! Mommy!" I feel Michelle's arms wrap around me. Looking down, I see she is crying.

Kneeling, I pull her into my arms, then hold her at arm's length and look her over for visible injuries.

"I'm so sorry, Dr. Shipman. She isn't hurt. Another child told her she needed to be in the baby room. Unfortunately, Michelle isn't the only child he's bullied. We have scheduled a meeting with his parents. We brought her out here to look at the art on the walls to take her mind off of what happened."

Relief, then anger passes through me. How dare any child be that way. I hope this doesn't negatively affect Michelle and make her not want to come back.

"Thank you for making her feel better." I scoop her into my arms and stand. "How about a vanilla bean Frappuccino? Will that make you feel better?"

Her frown is quickly replaced with a smile as she wipes the tears from her face. "Starbucks makes everything better."

The relief quickly vanishes when I turn and see Mitch staring at us, eyes wide, mouth open. I'm not ready to get into this with him.

"Bye, Ms. Tina. Mommy is taking me to Starbucks. Thanks for making me feel better."

She smiles. "Bye, sweet girl. I'll see you tomorrow."

Michelle turns her head and notices Mitch staring at us. She smiles as he slowly walks toward us. I have no idea how he will react to the fact I'm a mother. Not to mention I named her Michelle, the name we said we were going to name our first daughter. Butterflies swirl around in my stomach when he stops just inches from us and smiles at Michelle.

"Who do we have here?"

"I'm Michelle. My mommy is a doctor. Are you one of her patients? We are new here and need to make friends."

Floor, please open up and swallow me whole.

"Michelle?" he says and looks at me with what appears to be hurt in his eyes. "This is your mommy?"

"Yes. She's a doctor. I don't have a daddy."

I stifle a groan. And I just thought things couldn't get worse.

"Well, Michelle, it's very nice to meet you. I've known your mommy for a very long time."

"Do you want to get some Starbucks with us? Mommy says Starbucks makes everything better." She cocks her head at him. "You seem like you're sad."

He grins down at her. "I'm not sad, sweetheart. I just wasn't expecting to meet you today."

I can feel the unspoken questions radiating off of him. I can't do this. "Michelle, Mr. Davis is a very busy man. I'm sure he doesn't have time to join us."

Mitch looks at me, then Michelle again, a radiant smile crossing his face. "I can't say no to such a cute little thing. I'd love to join you and your mommy."

"See, Mommy. He wants Starbucks, too." Michelle squirms in my arms, so I set her down.

She reaches up and takes our hands, pulling us toward Starbucks. "What's your favorite drink? I like the vanilla bean Frap. It's hard for me to say the long word. I also love the lemony cake. It's so yummy."

"I like the lemony cake, too. It was my mother's favorite. But I usually get just plain coffee." He looks at me. "How old is she?"

"Almost three." I look down at Michelle, who's still talking, and smirk. "She is too smart and precocious for her own good."

"Her vocabulary blows me away."

Michelle releases our hands and runs to the counter, jumping up and down as she looks into the glass display case with all the treats. She begins to chant, "Lemony cake. Lemony cake. Lemony cake."

The barista chuckles. "You wouldn't happen to want a piece of lemon loaf, would you?"

"Yes, and a vanilla bean Frap, too, please," she says excitedly.

"What do your mommy and daddy want to drink?"

"I don't have a daddy. Just a mommy."

The barista's cheeks heat. "I'm... I'm so sorry. I just assumed."

I smile. "No worries. I'll take a—"

Mitch interrupts. "She'll take a venti skinny mocha, and I'll have a venti Pike Place."

"Mitch..." I place my hands on my hips, "I can order my own drink."

"I know what you drink. Plus, it's my treat. It's not every day I get to meet your daughter for the first time." Hurt laces his voice.

He pulls his phone from his pocket and scans the Starbucks app, leaving no room for discussion.

CHAPTER 13

~Mitch~

To say I almost fell over when Michelle called Jayna mommy is an understatement. But with those wild black curls, emerald eyes, and button nose with a smattering of freckles, the resemblance is remarkable. To top it off, her name is Michelle. That was going to be *our* child's name. How could she name some other man's child Michelle?

Because you're the asshole who left her. That's how.

And no father? What kind of a man doesn't claim his own child?

What a little spitfire she is, and smart. My heart just about burst when she said she loved the *lemony cake.* I can't help but wonder if this is my mom working her magic from heaven, trying to soften my heart. She was addicted to lemon loaf. Jayna and I ate many a piece with my mother.

Jayna places a hand on her heart and looks at me, as if she knows what I'm thinking, then gasps when the barista refers to us as Michelle's parents.

I'm not that lucky.

I frown. Where the hell did that thought come from? I'm not worthy of love from an innocent child. The people I love the most always leave me.

When my name is called, I hand Michelle her lemon loaf, then hand Jayna their drinks. When I turn to grab mine, I feel tugging on my pant leg. I look down at Michelle's face, my heart clenching.

"Thank you for my Frap and lemony cake. Would you like to sit with me and mommy?"

Jayna opens her mouth, but before she can say anything, I squat down to Michelle's level. "Not this time, sweetheart. I have to be somewhere, but maybe we can meet again sometime soon."

She hugs my neck with one arm, keeping a tight hold on her lemon loaf with the other. "I'd like that, Mr. Davis."

"You can call me Mitch." I tap her on the nose and stand.

"Hey, our names sound the same." She giggles. "Michelle and Mitch."

"They sure do. How about that." I look at Jayna.

She looks away, but before she does, I see pain in her eyes. The same pain that is probably reflected in mine.

"Goodbye, Jayna. See you later, Michelle. It was so nice to meet you."

"Bye, Mr. Mitch."

I rush out the door like my ass is on fire. I can't process all this. Does my dad know Jayna has a child? If so, I'm going to be pissed that he didn't tell me.

As soon as I get into my car, I call my dad.

"Hello, son. How was your afternoon?"

"Eventful," I grit out.

He pauses. "What's wrong?"

"Jayna has a daughter. Did you know?"

"What? Jayna is a mother?" There's no mistaking the surprise in his voice.

"You mean to tell me you had no clue she has a two-year-old little girl?"

"I haven't seen or spoken to her parents in years. Not since after your mother died. Now that I'm in Arkansas, I rarely make it back to Ohio. I didn't realize she had a family of her own."

"She has a daughter but evidently no *baby daddy.*"

"Mitch," my dad admonishes, "you don't have to be so crass. What makes you say that anyway."

"*I* didn't say it. Her *daughter* did."

"No daddy? That just breaks my heart. Every child needs a father."

"And the biggest kicker? Her name's Michelle."

"Michelle? Isn't that—"

I interrupt. "The name we always said we would name our daughter? It is."

"It sounds like she was thinking of you and wished you were the father. Unfortunately, you threw that away due to your fear. More than anything, I regret the way my reaction to the loss of your mother affected you."

"Stop, Dad. That's not why. It's just the way I am."

He snorts. "Who do you think you're kidding? You loved Jayna, cherished her, the same way I did your mom. It was a beautiful thing to see."

"Well, I'm not that person anymore."

"You can be, son, if you just open your heart."

I shake my head, suddenly exhausted. "I don't feel up to talking about this anymore, Dad. I need to get home and have a drink. And before you can say anything, no, I'm not going to drink myself stupid. But you have to promise me we won't discuss this when I get there."

"I won't say anything. You know I'm the last person to judge. I have Chinese takeout and beer ready and waiting. I won't say another word unless you bring it up."

"Thanks, Dad. See you in a bit."

CHAPTER 14

~Jayna~

I was very thankful Mitch couldn't stay. I didn't know why he looked so hurt, almost like I betrayed him. He was the one who broke up with me, not the other way around.

I look at Michelle, laughing when I see her face and shirt covered in lemon loaf crumbs. "Did you think it was going to run away from you?" I tease.

"Mommy, cake can't run away. I just gobbled it down like the Cookie Monster gobbles down cookies. Yum, yum, yum." She giggles.

"I think you could give the Cookie Monster a run for his cookies," I chuckle.

She stops eating and looks thoughtful. "I like that man, Mommy. He was nice, and when you looked at him, your eyes sparkled."

I blink, frowning. "They did?"

"Yes. You looked both happy and sad. Were you sad?"

What do I say to that? "Well... I just haven't seen Mr. Davis in a long time. That may be why I seemed both happy and sad."

"No need to be sad. You can see him now and be his friend again."

I shake my head, smirking. "Are you ready to go home, squirt?"

"Yes. I'm all better."

"That's good. Let's get home and take a bubble bath. How's that sound?"

Michelle jumps off the chair. "I love the bubbles. They make me smell like peaches."

"They make you smell good enough to eat," I say and tickle her sides.

After I pull out my phone and order an Uber, we head to the door.

"Remember, you need to hold my hand once we get outside." Between the people rushing around and the cars speeding down the street, I'm terrified something will happen to her.

Luckily, we don't have to wait too long for our car, a late-model Honda Accord with a car seat, to pull up. After buckling Michelle in, I settle into the back seat, sighing. It's been a long, stressful day seeing Benson, then Mitch, *twice*. Not to mention Mitch seeing Michelle before I was ready.

The Uber driver looks into the rearview mirror. "There's a wreck up ahead, so it may take us longer to get you two home. Do you care if I turn on some country music?"

"Not at all."

I hand Michelle my phone and headphones, then close my eyes and relax. When the song "What Could've Been" by Gone West starts, I have to fight back the tears. I turn my head and stare out the window so Michelle doesn't see. All I can think about is what if Mitch would have stayed? Where would we be in our lives right now?

The Uber driver smiles sadly at me with a knowing look on her face, like she's experienced something similar. "Traffic is moving. I should have you home in no time."

I manage to smile. "Thank you."

Twenty minutes later, the Uber pulls up in front of our apartment, Michelle looking up from my phone when the car stops. "Thanks for the ride, miss," Michelle says in her sweet voice.

"You're very welcome. You were such a good girl. It was like you weren't even back there."

"I was listening to my music."

"It must've been some good music."

"It's the bestest."

I unbuckle the car seat, then help Michelle down so she can scoot over the back seat and out of the car. "Come on, baby. Time to get you into that bubble bath."

Earl, the doorman, opens the door as we approach. "Hello, Dr. Shipman, Princess Michelle. How was your day?"

"It was great, Earl, and I've told you that you don't have to call me doctor."

"Yes, I do, ma'am. You've earned that title."

"*Ma'am?*" I chuckle. "Now I feel old, too."

His face falls. "Oh... I'm sorry. I didn't mean to make you feel that way."

I wave him off. "Stop, Earl. I'm just messing with you."

"Mommy, stop messin' with Mr. Earl. He's my friend."

Earl smiles, then walks to his station and picks up a bouquet of flowers. "These came for you a few minutes ago. Would you like me to take them up for you?"

"That's not necessary. I think we can handle it." I hand Michelle my purse, then take the ostentatious flowers. These are too gaudy to be from Benson. My skin crawls when the realization of who they're probably from hits me.

Once we walk through our door, Michelle runs to her room to see her dolls. I pull the card from the flowers, holding my breath. It reeks of Preston's cologne. Do I even want to read it?

Jayna, I'm starting to grow impatient. You are all I seem to think about. Don't make me wait much longer. It won't do either of us any good. Yours~ P

It's suddenly hard to breathe. This feels like a threat. I don't know how to respond or what to do. Chills start to rack my body. I really have no one here that I know or trust well enough to talk to about it... other than Mitch. But would he even care?

All through dinner and Michelle's bath, my head is spinning. Should I reach out to Mitch? Will he think I'm being dramatic, just trying to get his attention? *Am* I trying to get his attention? I shouldn't want it after seeing how he treats women. Then again, seeing how he was with Michelle...

After her bath and bedtime story, Michelle quickly falls asleep. I walk into the kitchen, grab the flowers, and stuff them into the trash with a grimace. I don't want anything from that man.

Before I can second-guess myself, I pull out my phone and text the number I remember for Mitch. I have no idea if it still his number, but if it's not, I'll take that as a sign that I should just deal with this on my own.

Mitch, I hope this is still your number. This is Jayna. I need your help. Please, text me back.

To get my mind off things, I busy myself picking up the kitchen and living room.

My phone starts vibrating on the kitchen island with a call, not a text. Hand shaking, I see Mitch's number on the screen.

"Hello?"

"Jayna, what's wrong?"

"Thank you for getting back to me. I hate to bother you, but I just don't have anyone else I can call." Despite trying my hardest, my voice starts to quiver as I fight back tears. "It's one of the doctors I work with. He's really starting to step over the line and, quite frankly, freaking me out."

"What do you mean by stepping over the line?"

"He keeps hitting on me and is becoming more insistent. This morning, he cornered me when I got back from Starbucks, demanding to know where I'd been. When I got home tonight, there was a garish bouquet of flowers waiting for me."

"Are you sure they're from him?"

"Yes. The card was soaked in his cologne. That was creepy in and of itself, but what the note said sent chills down my spine."

"What did it say?" Mitch growled.

"He basically said he was tired of waiting for me to accept his offers of a date, that I'm all he can think about. The real kicker was when he said not to make him wait much longer because it won't do either one of us any good. I feel like that's a threat."

"That is most definitely a threat and can be considered workplace harassment. The first thing you need to do is notify HR that this is happening."

"But I'm afraid if I file charges, I'll have to find a new place to work. I love my job, Mitch."

"What he's doing is creepy and unprofessional. What if he did this to somebody else? You probably should've drawn a line that time you all went out after work."

I tighten my hand around my phone. "Are you *kidding* me right now? You're blaming *me* for this? I should've fucking known better than to ask for advice from the man whore."

I hang up and slam the phone down. What a total ass.

CHAPTER 15

~Mitch~

"Damn it," I bite out in exasperation and toss my phone down onto the couch. I knew that douche I'd seen her with was a creep, but he's taking it too far. Why did she have to encourage him? I know it was just to stick it to me after witnessing me with that woman in the lobby.

I need to apologize to Jayna, but I'm going to let her cool off first. From experience, I know she has to get her anger out of her system before she will listen to me.

From the recliner, Dad furrows his brows. "What was that about? It sounded like you were blaming Jayna for something that probably wasn't her fault."

I scrub a hand down my face. "I know. It just frustrates me that she put herself in that position."

"Back up and tell me what's going on."

"Jayna saw me being an ass to a woman I'd been with." Dad tilts his head, a knowing look in his eyes. "Don't look at me that way. You know my stance on relationships."

"Sadly, I do. Which I can't understand, but that's not the point. What did her seeing you being an ass have to do with that phone call?"

"That was the first time I'd seen her again. Later that day, I saw her in the lobby of our building with her co-workers. One of the doctors was all over her, and something about him just rubbed me the wrong way. I felt he was...off. I don't know how to explain it."

"I do. You still have feelings for Jayna and didn't like seeing another man pay attention to her."

I snort. "Whatever. That's the furthest thing from the truth."

"Keep telling yourself that, son." My dad smirks at me.

Fuck, he's not going to let this go, hopeless romantic that he is. "Anyway, later that night, we happened to be at the same bar and I saw her dancing with him. I think it gave him the wrong idea. Ever since, it seems he has taken an unhealthy interest in her. Tonight, he sent her flowers, the card basically telling her he was done waiting on her to accept his invitation to dinner and she'd better agree if she knows what's good for her."

Saying it out loud makes my blood boil. I need to call Jayna back.

Dad glares at me, as if I'm the dumbest guy around. "Let me get this straight. You just blamed *Jayna* for some psychopath threatening her? Your mother and I taught you better than that, Mitch. You can deny it all you want, but you still love her. In fact, you never stopped. Fear ambushed your heart, turning you cold to anyone you think might cause you pain. That is why you treat women the way you do. *Damn it,* son. Jayna isn't just any woman, and you know it."

"I know. I feel horrible. Let's eat, then I'll call her back and try to get her to forgive me."

"I wouldn't blame her if she told you to jump off a bridge."

"More like fuck off."

* * *

I called and texted Jayna several times last night, getting no response. It had pissed me off, but Dad was quick to point out that it was my fault.

I'll just have to try and intercept her when she gets to the building. I know she has a hard time functioning without her morning coffee, so if I can catch her in Starbucks, maybe I can convince her to hear me out.

I glance at my watch and see that it's seven thirty. If I don't hurry, Jayna will beat me to the office.

After the fastest shower humanly possible, I'm dressed and out the door in under twenty minutes. I whip in and out of traffic, driving like an asshole, if the honks are any indication. The damn parking garage already filling up, I have to drive up three levels. Not waiting on the elevator, I run down the stairs and out the door...almost getting run over by a group of dogs and their human. It looks like the same group that ran into Jayna on her first day here.

Smiling my apology, I rush into the office building. People walk in and out of Starbucks, but there's no sign of Jayna. Hopefully I haven't missed her.

"Good morning, Mr. Davis. Do you want your usual?"

"Good morning. Yes, I'll take my usual, plus a skinny mocha. Make them both venti, please."

Just as I grab the cups from the barista, Jayna walks in and stops short. When she glares at me, I see hurt and anger on her face.

I hold up her drink. "Peace offering. You look like you could use it. Please, hear me out."

A little surprised, the corner of her lip twitches as she grabs her cup. "Peace offering, huh? It's going to take more than my favorite drink to make me forget you treated me like crap."

I sigh. "I know. I tried to call you last night, numerous times, but you ignored all my calls."

"I have a small child, Mitch. We both fell asleep in my bed after reading a bedtime story. I saw your calls and texts this morning. Quite frankly, I wanted you to think about what you did, know how much it hurt. As far as needing coffee, it goes hand-in-hand with said small child. If you would've gotten here about fifteen minutes ago, you would've heard her screaming out her *need* for Starbucks this morning."

We walk over to the nearest table and sit. I laugh at Jayna's exaggerated eye roll. "Your daughter is adorable. I think you may have created the world's youngest coffee addict."

I sigh. "Listen, Jayna, I know it was a very shitty thing for me to say to you. Believe me. Dad was quick to tell me the same thing." I smile. "I swear, he loves you more than he loves me. We both want to kick that douche's ass. If you want to file a complaint against him for sexual harassment, I will help you. Just because I'm a divorce lawyer doesn't mean I don't help my friends with other types of legal matters."

She cocks her head. "Friends? Is that what we are? I'd love for us to be *friends* again. I miss you, Mitch."

"Of course we're friends. I've missed you, too."

"Did your dad mention he asked me to dinner tonight?"

"Yes, he did." I smirk. "He ordered me to be on my best behavior. Do you have somebody to watch Michelle?"

"Yes. Rebekah's sister is going to watch her for me."

"You are welcome to bring her if you'd like."

Jayna's eyes widen slightly in surprise. I can't believe I just said that. Finding out about her still stings my ego. I know she's been with other men since me, but I don't like thinking about it.

I drain the rest of my coffee, looking at my watch. "I need to get up to my office. I have a conference call in twenty minutes. Are you headed to your office?"

She shakes her head. "Not just yet. I need to ready myself to face Dr. Joseph. It was his day to come in for the early patients. My first patient isn't until nine, so that gives me about twenty more minutes to avoid him. I'll see you later, Mitch."

"Try to stay away from that creep, Jayna. If you need to, you can text or call me anytime. You have my number. See ya tonight."

I walk out, a spring in my step. This feels good. *Too* good. Not able to stop myself, I look back over my shoulder. Jayna's smiling wistfully at an elderly couple holding hands across the small table. This sends a pang to my heart, causing it to beat a little faster.

* * *

"Good morning, Mitch," Margaret says brightly as I step off the elevator. Then she narrows her eyes at me. "Are you okay? You look, well...happy."

I place a hand on my chest, acting wounded. "Margaret, that hurts. Aren't I always happy?"

"Don't give me that. The aura around you is brighter today."

I place a hand on her desk and lean forward, lowering my voice. "Tell ya what. I'll do my best to keep it that way, just for you." Smiling, I stand straight again. "Do I have any messages? I'm expecting a call from Mrs. Taylor's lawyer this morning."

"Nothing has come in yet, but I'll buzz you as soon as it does."

"Thanks, Margaret. I'll be in my office."

When I pass by Mr. Burns' office, I see him talking on the phone, a scowl on his face. I slow my steps and listen in, hoping it doesn't have to do with the Taylor case.

"You heard me, son. I don't want a repeat of Amber. I have too much to do to be getting your ass out of another mess." He slams down the phone.

Quickly, I walk to my office and shut my door. I think I'll wait to talk to Mr. Burns until I have some good news to bring him.

As if on cue, my phone buzzes. I press the button.

"Mr. Smith is on the phone for you. Line two."

"Thank you, Margaret."

Taking a deep breath, I pick up the phone. "Mr. Smith, thank you for getting back to me so quickly. My client would really like to put all of this behind him and move on."

"As does my client. It took a lot of convincing, but she has agreed to the terms of the settlement. I advised her that your offer was more than fair, especially in light of the indisputable video evidence you presented."

"I do believe Mr. Taylor was more than fair. Once she signs the papers, please have them sent to the office."

"They are being sent over as we speak. Have a nice day, Mr. Davis."

"You, too, Mr. Smith."

There's no stopping the smile spreading across my face. I pick up my cell and text Jayna.

Hey. Well, they agreed to the settlement. Looks like I'll soon be junior partner. I just had to share with someone, and you were the first person I thought of.

Her response is almost immediate.

I'm so happy for you, Mitch. I know how hard you've worked. Tonight will be a celebration :)

We will definitely be celebrating, Jayna :)

How is it that years have passed, but just after a couple of weeks, she's the first person I think about? In my head, I know why. I just buried my feelings under layers of pain and fear. I wish I could be the man she needs, but I know I'm not worthy of her.

Pushing up from my desk, I head to Mr. Burns' office to share the good news. I hope it will improve his mood.

His door is shut, but not completely. I raise my hand to knock, but I feel a slap on my shoulder, Mr. Jefferson standing there, smile on his face.

"Good morning, Mitch. How's everything going with the Taylor case?"

"Good morning, Mr. Jefferson. That's actually why I was about to knock on Mr. Burns' door. I have news."

He gestures to the door. "Then let's go in. Samuel is in there with Maxon. You can share it with us all." He knocks lightly and opens the door, waving me in. "Look who I ran into in the hallway. He says he has news on the Taylor case."

Mr. Burns smiles brightly. "Come in, my boy, and give us the news."

"I just got off the phone with Don Smith, Mrs. Taylor's lawyer. She has agreed to everything. They are sending the papers over as we speak."

Mr. Burns slaps his hands on his desk and stands. "This is great news. Well done, Mitch. I think we need to celebrate. After all, we have to welcome our new junior partner in style." He opens his desk drawer and pulls out a folder, handing it to me. "From the first day you started at this firm, I knew you were a star in the making. You have proven yourself over and over again. This is another shining example of how you do whatever it takes to give our clients what they deserve. We are all so proud of you. Take a look at this paperwork, then we'll all meet for lunch and make it official."

"Great job, Mitch," both Spencer Jefferson and Samuel Toone say.

Mr. Toone holds out his hand. "I knew you were the perfect choice for junior partner."

"Thank you, sir. I'm truly honored. I'm going to give Mr. Taylor a call and share the good news."

Mr. Burns walks me to the door. "Meet us at the country club at noon."

Margaret, hearing the commotion in the office, looks at me as I walk out. Her smile matches mine as she waves me over. "Get over here, boy, and let me give you a hug. I knew you would get it done."

"Boy?" I chuckle.

"You're like a son to me, Mitch."

"Thank you, Margaret. You've always been there for me when I needed you. Just like a mother. You even keep me in line."

I can feel a mother's love in her hug. Even six years later, I still miss my mother's hug. I swallow and blink back the tears threatening to form in my eyes.

Clearing my throat, I step back. "I'll be in my office. If I get any calls, take a message. Unless it's an emergency."

"Sure thing, Mitch. Again, congratulations."

I wink and walk away.

CHAPTER 16

~Jayna~

The smile doesn't leave my face as I walk to my office. Mitch did seem sincere when he apologized for being such a dick last night. I'm looking forward to dinner with him and Benson tonight.

My mood quickly dissolves when I open my office door and see Preston sitting at my desk, a scowl on his face.

"What are you doing in my office?"

"Don't look so shocked to see me. I didn't hear from you last night and want to know what you thought of the flowers I sent you. It was just rude to not call and thank me. I was hoping you'd thank me properly this morning." He waggles his eyebrows, making me want to throw up.

"What?" I ask, aghast. "First, I had a child I needed to get ready for bed. Second, the flowers were not necessary, and honestly, I didn't appreciate you sending them to my home."

"Not necessary? You give flowers to those you care about. I care about you."

"You don't even *know* me, Preston. We've only been acquainted less than three weeks. Quite frankly, you're making me uncomfortable. I have told you several times that I'm not interested in going out with you. Now, please..." I sweep my arm to the door, "leave my office."

"We will discuss this more later."

He stands and walks out the door, leaving me in a state of shock and completely speechless. It's like he doesn't hear a single word I say and is living in his own fantasy world. Something is not right with that man.

Rebekah peeks her head into my office. "Good morning, Jayna. Your nine o'clock is here to see you. Exam room two. Be ready. It's a gnarly ingrown toenail."

I scrunch up my face. "Thanks. Just what I want to deal with first thing in the morning. I'm glad I only had coffee for breakfast. Let her know I'll be right in."

"Sure thing. Are you okay? You seem a bit...off."

"I'm fine. Just had something weird happen this morning."

"Well, I'm here if you need to talk."

"Thanks. I appreciate that."

Thank goodness we were slammed with patients. I didn't have any time to think about Mr. Creepy. Except for a few times in the hallway when he made it a point to touch or brush against me when he passed, even though I plastered my body against the wall, I was able to avoid him. Bek saw him do it one time, her eyes wide as she looked at me, a concerned expression crossing her face.

We need to talk, she mouthed. I just nodded.

Deciding to leave my notes for the morning, I duck out early, not even telling anybody. I just don't want to risk getting accosted by

Preston. Besides, I want to spend some time with Michelle before going out tonight and leaving her with Bek's sister.

When I get to Michelle's classroom, all the kids are sitting on the floor, watching a Disney sing-along video. I smile when I see Michelle singing at the top of her lungs. She jumps up and runs into my arms.

"Mommy, you're here early. You never come during sing-along time."

"I know, sweetheart, but I wanted to spend some time with you before I go out to dinner tonight. Do you remember me telling you that Rebekah's sister, Cammy, is going to watch you for a couple of hours?"

"Yes. You said she'd be a lot of fun. I like Rebekah, so I know I'll like her sister, too."

I sign Michelle out, then we go to Chick-Fil-A for dinner. After she eats and I let her play for a bit, I stand. "It's time to go, honey. We need to get home and take a bath before Cammy comes over."

"One more time down the slide, please?"

I smile. "Okay. Just one more."

She goes down one more time, then puts on her shoes.

"Did you see me slide down the big slide all by myself? I'm not scared anymore. I'm a big girl. I put my shoes on all by myself, too." She stretches out her legs. "Tie my shoes, please, Mommy."

I pat my knee. "Put your foot here and I'll fix you right up."

"That's because you're a fixer. That's what doctors do. They fix."

"We sure try. Come on. Our Uber's here."

"Can I have a piggyback ride to the car?"

I squat down so she can climb onto my back. "Your chariot awaits, m'lady."

She giggles all the way to the car, the sound music to my ears.

CHAPTER 17

~Mitch~

To say Mr. Taylor was thrilled with the settlement was an understate-ment. He said it was worth every penny to get her lying, cheating hooks out of him. The big bonus he gave me was an unexpected surprise, too. Lunch with the partners was filled with drinks and good food, Mr. Taylor even joining us for a bit. I still can't believe I'm a junior partner before thirty.

After lunch, I head back to the office, the rest of the partners calling it a day. I haven't done much this afternoon except respond to a few emails and make a couple of phone calls.

When I look at my watch, I see it's four fifteen. I wonder if I can catch Jayna before she leaves for the day. She didn't respond to the text I sent a few minutes ago, making me think she's probably with a patient. Dad wants us to pick her up and drive her to dinner instead of her taking an Uber.

When I head down to her office, one of the nurses I saw with

Jayna the other day sits at the reception desk. She smiles. "Hi. Can I help you?"

"I hope so. I'm here to see Dr. Shipman. I'm Mitch Davis, an old friend of hers. I don't have an appointment. I just need to talk to her for a moment."

Her smile widens. "I'm sorry, Mr. Davis. She's already left for the day. She texted a few minutes ago saying she was picking up her daughter a little early to take her out to get something to eat."

"I guess that's why she hasn't returned my text."

"I'm sure she'll text you back as soon as she sees it." She chuckles. "Michelle likes to have all of her attention. Jayna is a wonderful mother."

"I always knew she would be." That nagging pain hits me in the chest again. "Thanks for letting me know."

Just as I'm about to leave, Dr. Douche walks up and looks me over. "We aren't taking any more patients today. Come back in the morning."

How rude. I wonder if he acts like this to everyone, or if it's just me.

Before I can say anything, the nurse turns to him. "Mitch is here to see Jayna. She told me she's having dinner with him and his father tonight."

What looks to be anger flashes through his eyes. "Jayna is having dinner with you tonight?"

I smile. "Yes, she is. We go *way* back." Not that it's any of his damn business.

"That's funny. I didn't think she knew anybody in Texas."

"Well, I've known Jayna since we were teenagers." I turn back to the nurse. "It was nice talking to you." I don't even acknowledge Dr. Douche as I turn and walk out the door.

That man sets my hairs on end. There's something off about him. I'm relieved Jayna saw through him.

When I get home, Dad is on the phone with my little sister,

Emily. He gives me a smile and a wave, telling her I just walked through the door. He holds out the phone.

"Your sister wants to talk to you."

Smiling, I take the phone. "Hi, peanut. When are you going to come see me?"

"Mitch, I miss you. I was mad Daddy went to see you without me. I have my dance recital next month, so Mommy said I needed to stay home and practice. You know I'm the best."

"You have a dance recital next month?"

"Yes, and I have the lead."

"That's my girl. You be sure and let me know the date and time. I promise to come see you. I wouldn't miss it for anything."

"I can't wait to see you. Henry and Kristi will be there, too. Did you know I'm going to be an aunt? Kristi is having a baby."

"I know. I'm going to be an uncle. How exciting, right?

"I'm going to put Dad back on the phone. I love you, peanut. See you next month."

"I love you, too, Mitch. Bye."

I hand Dad the phone, a huge smile on his face. He is the proudest dad on earth.

I decide to grab a quick shower while Dad finishes up talking to Emily and Marley. As soon as I get to the bedroom, my phone buzzes. I smile, seeing Jayna's name on my screen.

Sorry I missed your text. Michelle had me running like crazy in Chick-Fil-A. I'd love it if you would come pick me up. I'll be ready.

No problem. Send me your address and we'll be there around 7.

I leave my phone on my nightstand and head into the bathroom. Ever since running into Dr. Douche, my muscles have been tense. A hot shower will help me relax. I turn it on and strip out of my suit, leaving my clothes on the floor. The minute I step under the hot steam, I feel some of the tension drain away.

A vision of Jayna, naked, comes unbidden into my mind. I can't stop my body's reaction to it, either. I palm myself and start stroking slowly. She was gorgeous as a teenager, but she is absolutely stunning now. The changes to her body since she had a child have only made her look more magnificent. Full hips, fuller breasts... She's every man's dream. Picturing her naked and soapy has me exploding in seconds.

I take a few minutes to calm down, then quickly wash myself. I'm pathetic. And need to get laid. Maybe I'll call Luke and see if he wants to hit up some bars tomorrow. I can't keep lusting over Jayna. But somehow, the thought of hitting up the bar to find a willing woman doesn't have the same appeal it used to.

After I get dressed in my charcoal gray Armani suit, I walk into the living room, seeing Dad watching the news. "Well, don't you look handsome, son. Tell me. Are you trying to impress someone?" He raises his eyebrows.

"I *always* look handsome. After all, I am your son."

He laughs. "We do clean up nicely. So, are we picking up Jayna or is she meeting us at the restaurant?"

"We're picking her up. She just texted me her address. It's not far. I told her we'd be there around seven."

"Sounds good. Marley was sad she didn't get a chance to talk to you."

"I'll have to give her a call. I plan on seeing Emily dance next month. It will be good to see everyone."

"Maybe Jayna and her daughter would like to come, too."

I sigh. "Don't you think you are assuming a lot, Dad. She doesn't even know us anymore."

"How can you say that, son? She's always been one of us. Open your eyes...or your heart."

"Dad," I moan. "Just stop. I know you are a true believer in love and fate, but that's just not me."

"Whatever you say. Just keep telling yourself that."

"Let's just go."

We take the Tesla...I know Dad will buy Marley one of these just so he can drive it...to Jayna's apartment, less than ten minutes away. Arriving early, we decide to park and go up to get her.

Dad looks around, impressed. "This is a nice building. Jayna has done well for herself."

"I always knew she would. She is one stubborn, determined woman."

"She reminded me so much of your mother. They were two peas in a pod."

That thought causes another crack in the wall around my heart. "Yes, they were." I smile sadly. "Sometimes I thought Mom loved her more than she loved me."

"She was the daughter she never had, but she loved you more than anything. After all, you were her firstborn."

Jayna must have told the doorman she was expecting us because he directs us to apartment 1502.

Taking the elevator up, we walk off when it stops on her floor. Before I can knock, the door flies open, Michelle standing there, a curious expression on her face. I can hear Jayna in the background.

"What have I told you about opening the door without me?"

"Hi, Mr. Mitch. Do you remember me? My name's Michelle." She looks over at Dad. "He looks like you."

"Hi, Michelle. Of course I remember you. This is my dad, Benson."

Dad's eyes sparkle when he kneels down to Michelle's level. "Aren't you just the prettiest little thing ever." He opens his arms for a hug. "You look just like your mommy."

I suck in a breath when Jayna walks up. She wears black dress pants and an emerald green silk blouse that makes her eyes pop, which glisten with tears when she watches Michelle hug dad.

"Michelle, I put *Frozen* on in your playroom. You can watch it with Cammy before you go to bed. Cammy is in there waiting on you. I love you so much. Be a good girl."

"I love you, too, Mommy. And I'm always a good girl."

"Yes, you are."

She smiles, waving over her shoulder as she skips away. "Bye, Mr. Mitch and Mr. Benson."

Dad looks at Jayna. "You've done such a good job with her. She is so sweet and polite. My Emily would just love to play with her."

"Thank you, Benson. It can be really hard sometimes, but she is such a wonderful child. I'm very lucky."

"So... Where does everyone want to go for dinner?" I ask.

"I'm in the mood for a good steak," Dad says. "I've heard Pappas Brothers Steakhouse is the best. Is that okay with you two? I sure hope so, because I already took the liberty to make reservations."

"That's fine with me. You know I love a good steak. Jayna?"

"Steak sounds good to me, too. I've heard their cheesecake is to die for. One of my patients mentioned it the other day when she found out I was new to the area." Jayna walks out and closes the door.

"Then we must get cheesecake for dessert." Dad pats his eight-pack. "I'll just work out extra hard tomorrow."

Jayna rolls her eyes. "Benson, I'm sure you could miss a workout or ten and still be fit as a teenager."

"Emily keeps me on my toes." He smirks. "I have to stay in shape to keep up with her. It's different being a dad to a four-year-old at almost fifty as opposed to my early twenties."

"You're right. It's all I can do to keep up with Michelle now. I couldn't imagine doing it when I'm fifty."

I call for the elevator, which opens immediately. "I don't know about y'all, but I'm starving. Shall we go?" I wave my hand toward the open elevator doors.

"Yes. Let's eat." Dad steps to the side and looks at Jayna, sweeping his arm toward the elevator. "Ladies first."

When we enter the lobby, her doorman wishing us a good evening, I usher her outside with my hand on her lower back, Dad leading the way. I have to admit, this feels right...too right. I can feel the electricity passing between us, and it's almost more than I can take. I know Jayna feels it, too, because her sharp intake of breath when I touched her was a sure tell.

I stop in front of the rental. "Dad lucked out and got a parking space right out front. Can you believe that?"

"Is that a Tesla?"

"Yes. Marley wants one, so Dad decided to rent one while he's here to see if it lives up to the hype. I think he's going to buy one for her and drive it himself."

Dad snorts. "I am buying it for Marley, but I can enjoy driving it, too, can't I?"

"I bet you won't see too many Teslas around Arkansas."

"Shows what you know, my boy. Marley is so intrigued by them because she's seen several of them driving around."

Jayna bursts out laughing. "You just got told."

I smirk and open the front passenger door. "After you." After I close her door, I manage to squish myself into the back seat, which was not made for a man over six feet tall.

Dad and Jayna fall into easy conversation, just like no time has passed at all. I must admit, it makes me a little jealous. We don't have that camaraderie anymore.

Thank goodness Dad made reservations because this place is packed. Once we sit, the waitress takes our drink order and rushes off to fill it.

"Everything on here looks delicious," Jayna remarks, looking at the menu. "I thought I wanted steak, but the seafood looks delectable, too."

"Then get the Filet Duo," Dad suggests. "It's the best of both worlds. I think that's what I'm going to order."

"So much food…" She smiles. "But I think you've twisted my arm."

"I'm going for the ten-ounce filet mignon with roasted wild mushrooms."

"Yum. I may have to sneak a mushroom."

Dad laughs. "You always did eat off of both our plates. I see some things haven't changed."

The waitress sets down our drinks, takes our food order, then rushes away. Jayna raises her glass. "To Mitch, for making junior partner at his firm. What a big accomplishment."

Dad is next. "To Mitch. I'm so proud of you, son. I know your mother is smiling down on you right now. Especially since you are celebrating with Jayna."

Well, this is awkward. What do I say to that? I clear my throat. "Thanks, Jayna, Dad. It means a lot."

I gulp my Macallan, while Jayna sips her champagne and Dad drinks his seltzer water with lime. After falling into drunkenness after Mom died, he chooses not to drink alcohol at all.

"So, son, when will everything be official?" he asks.

"As soon as I buy into the firm. I have an appointment with my financial advisor next week."

"How are the other associates going to take it now that you've been made junior partner?"

"I think most will be happy for me. I'm sure a few of the guys who have been with the firm for a while will be a little upset. I can't let that bother me. I've worked my ass off to make partner."

"Yes, you have. You've always been determined to get what you want." Dad glances at Jayna. "Don't forget all your life plans."

Cheeks reddening, she looks down and takes a sip of her champagne.

Not knowing what to say, I'm thankful when our waitress walks up, plates in hand.

"This smells like heaven. Dig in," Dad says with a laugh.

I'm starving, so I take a hearty bite. "This is delicious. You can cut this filet with a fork."

Jayna reaches over and stabs one of my mushrooms with her fork, smiling as she pops it into her mouth. "Yummy."

Seeing a drip of sauce on her bottom lip, I have the sudden urge to reach over and remove it with my thumb. She slowly licks her bottom lip, clearing off the sauce. I groan inwardly. My pants have suddenly become uncomfortable.

"So, Jayna, how's your job going? Do you like Dallas?" Dad asks, making us both startle and swing our gazes to him.

"I am loving Dallas so far. I love my job..." She sighs, "but one of the doctors I work with is a little on the creepy side. I'm sure he's harmless, but he's insistent I go out with him. I'm not interested. Besides, I will *never* date someone I work with."

Something about the way she says it, the biting tone of her voice, makes me believe she must be referring to Michelle's father.

Dad looks at her, concerned. "If you feel uncomfortable, maybe you should report him." He looks at me. "Is there any action she can take?"

"She can file sexual harassment charges."

"I'm not ready to do that just yet. If he does anything else, I will. I just hate to start something a few weeks into the job."

"You should always feel safe at your workplace." Dad takes another bite of food.

I nod. "You have to protect yourself. Remember, I am in the building if you need me."

"Thank you, Mitch."

Dad and Jayna exchange stories about things that have happened over the years, and the mood at the table lifts from heavy to light. I feel a bit like an outsider, but I like seeing my dad so happy.

While they are busy talking, the waitress starts to clear our plates, and I order a piece of cheesecake with chocolate on top. When it arrives, it's the biggest piece of cheesecake I've ever seen.

Jayna's eyes widen. "I'm stuffed, but how can I pass up something that looks so delicious?"

Dad smiles. "I second that."

The waitress places extra spoons on the table. "Can I get you folks anything else?"

We all shake our heads.

"Just the check," Dad replies.

She lays it on the table next to Dad. "You can pay when you're ready. No rush."

"It's a good thing the waitress brought extra spoons." I hand them out, and we all dig in.

After several minutes, Jayna slumps back in her chair and pats her stomach. "I feel like I'm about to burst at the seams. I'll probably fall asleep on the way home."

"You can fall asleep, and I won't even make fun of you for drooling," Dad teases.

Jayna swats his arm. "I don't drool."

I poke her in the side. "I remember a time you fell asleep on my lap and left a wet spot. Don't tell me you don't drool."

After paying for dinner, we stand and head for the door. Molly, the bartender I had sex with in my car, walks in with another woman.

She stops and places a hand on her hip. "Well, I guess they'll let anyone in here. I thought a nice restaurant like this wouldn't let man whores through the door."

I don't say anything as I walk out the door, but the look of pity and sadness on Jayna's face, as well as the disappointment on Dad's, says it all. The playful mood of the evening is definitely gone.

Nobody says much on the way home. Dad pulls up in front of Jayna's.

"I can walk myself in. Thank you for dinner, Benson. It was so good to see you again." She looks at me. "Congratulations again, Mitch. You've worked hard for this. I really am happy for you." She climbs out, leaving the door open for me to climb up front, rushing inside without looking back.

I climb into the passenger seat, feeling my dad's gaze on me. "Don't say a word, Dad. You can't say anything I'm not already thinking myself."

"Son..."

"Don't."

He sighs, pulling away from the curb. "I'm headed back to Arkansas tomorrow. I think I have things straightened out at the gym. If you continue to see things that don't seem right, let me know. I'm hoping the new pilot project will cut down on a lot of the issues."

I look at him and blow out a breath. "I'm sorry. Honestly, I'm embarrassed. I'm not proud of how I handle relationships. But I never lead women into believing it is more than what it is."

"That's the problem, son. You aren't protecting your heart. You've convinced yourself this is how things are supposed to be. I know how I reacted to your mother's death really messed you up, but the longer you go without dealing with the hurt, the more you're going to hurt yourself. You need to remember what you used to want and try to get that back. I don't think it's as impossible as you believe. You just have to be willing to open yourself up and change your mindset."

"I think it's too late for me."

"It's never too late. Just take it one day at a time. Prove to yourself, and Jayna, that you're still the man she fell in love with all those years ago. I still see the adoration in her eyes when she looks at you."

I snort. "A minute ago, all I saw was disgust."

"How did you expect her to feel?"

"I don't know, Dad. I haven't thought about anyone else's feelings for so long. All I know is that I don't like what I'm feeling right now."

"Follow your heart. As much as you don't want to accept it, it won't lead you wrong."

"Thanks for being here for me, Dad."

We pull up to my place just in time. The conversation was getting too heavy for me. We walk inside in companionable silence, smiling at a young couple walking off the elevator as we walk on.

I open the apartment and think about how quiet it will be when Dad leaves tomorrow. "What time is your flight?"

"Twelve thirty. I have to be at the airport by eleven."

"Do you want to meet for coffee beforehand? I should be free by ten."

"Of course. I'm going to stop by the gym, just to make sure everybody knows my expectations before I leave, then I'll meet you at Starbucks.

"I'm going to call Marley, then go to bed. I'll see you in the morning."

"Good night, Dad."

I strip out of my clothes and climb into bed, popping in my earbuds to listen to some music to help me relax. The song "Dear Today" by Luke Combs comes on, and I almost stop breathing from the weight of it on my chest.

I don't think sleep is going to find me any time soon.

CHAPTER 18

~Jayna~

Cammy is sitting on the couch watching tv when I open the door. "How was my girl?"

"She was absolutely perfect. So smart and funny. She kept me on my toes."

I laugh. "She's a mess. That's for sure. I'm so glad she was good for you."

"Did you have a nice dinner?"

"I did. The food was delicious." I smirk. "And I ate way too much of it."

Cammy smiles. "I'm glad you had a nice time. I'd be happy to watch Michelle any time you need me to."

"Wonderful. I'll be sure and take you up on that offer another time. Do you need me to call you an Uber?"

She stands and grabs her purse. "No, thanks. I drove."

I hand her some money as we walk to the door. "Please, drive home safely and text me to let me know when you get there."

"I will." She smiles as she walks out the door.

I plop down onto the couch, my thoughts running rampant. How I wish things were like they used to be, but I know that's a long shot. Especially after we ran into that woman at the restaurant, reminding me just how much Mitch has changed. It was like you could see his walls erecting over his heart the minute he saw her.

I text Benson, thanking him again for dinner, then on a whim, I decide to call Mitch.

It rings four times. Just as I'm about hang up, he answers.

"Jayna? Is everything okay?"

"Everything is fine. I just wanted to call and tell you how much I enjoyed tonight. I felt truly happy for the first time in a long time."

"Me, too." I hear him blow out a breath. "I wish I was the same person you fell in love with all those years ago, Jayna, but I'm not."

He hangs up before I can answer.

I whisper, "But you are. You just don't see it in yourself."

When my phone vibrates with an incoming text, my heart speeds up, hoping it's Mitch apologizing for hanging up on me. My stomach roils when I see a text from Dr. Creepy.

How was your date tonight? You won't go out with me, but you'll go out with the pretty boy lawyer? I saw you first!

My fingers fly over the keyboard.

Are you crazy?! This has got to stop! I don't want to report you for sexual harassment, but I will. Please don't speak to me again unless it has to do with a patient!!

I'm shaking. What the hell am I going to do? I like my job and don't want to have to find somewhere new for Michelle to go. She loves her daycare, but it's only for children of people who work in the building.

Needing someone else's opinion, I take a screenshot of the text and send it to Mitch.

WTF. He is mentally unstable. I will draw up a sexual harassment complaint in the morning and bring it up for you to look at and sign. The first thing you need to do tomorrow is go to HR and report this. Nobody should have to work in this kind of environment.

Thank you, Mitch. I had no one else to turn to.

You can always come to me.

And this is exactly why I know Mitch is finding his way back. This gives me the peace of mind to be able to fall asleep, in spite of Preston Joseph weighing on my mind.

* * *

I wake up, feeling little kisses all over my face. "Wake up, Mommy. I missed you so much last night. Did you have fun with Mr. Mitch and Mr. Benson? I had so much fun with Cammy. Can she come over again sometime?"

I rub my eyes. "Slow down, princess. I can only answer one question at a time."

As long as I have Michelle, I don't need an alarm clock. She is up at six thirty just about every day, unless I allow her to stay up later than her normal bedtime the night before.

"Sorry, Mommy," she giggles. "I'm just happy to see you."

"I'm happy to see you, too." I pull her down and give her a big hug. "To answer your questions, yes, I had a good time, and yes, Cammy can come over again. She told me she had so much fun with you. Thank you for being such a big girl."

"She was so nice and fun, but not as fun as you." She jumps up. "I'm hungry. Can I have some Cheerios with a banana?"

"You bet. Let's go."

We walk into the kitchen. I grab a bowl from the cabinet. "Do you want the banana cut up in your cereal, or do you want to eat it by itself?"

"I want it in my cereal. It's so good in milk."

"That's how I like mine, too." I smile, pouring the cereal, then cutting up the banana and pouring milk over it.

"Eat up, sweetie. We need to get dressed and get ready to go."

By the time I get to work, I'm a nervous wreck. I don't know how I'm going to be able to act normal around Preston and not have other people at the clinic know something is off. I take a big drink of my coffee to settle myself, then walk inside.

"Good morning, Jayna," Carrington greets me.

"Good morning, Carrington. You're sure chipper this morning."

He smiles. "That's because I met someone last night. He is just a dream." He leans closer and lowers his voice. "I think he may be the one I've been waiting for all my life."

It's good seeing my friend so happy. I'm glad someone is feeling lucky in love, and not nauseous from a stalker.

"Sounds like it was a night to remember."

He pauses and looks closely at me, cocking his head. "Are you okay, Jayna? You don't look like your usual self."

I laugh, waving a hand through the air nonchalantly. "I'm fine. I was just out later than usual and didn't get as much sleep."

He doesn't look convinced, but thankfully, he drops it. "Okay. Anyway, your first patient just canceled. So take a few minutes to enjoy that mocha while it's hot before your next one arrives. You know Mary will send them back as soon as they get here. She likes to keep the patients flowing so we don't have to stay late."

"That she does, but I like it. It makes the day go by faster."

"True, but sometimes I like the fifteen-minute breather when someone cancels."

"Have you seen Rebekah?" I glance around. "I wanted to tell her how much Michelle loved Cammy."

"She was in the break room eating her breakfast."

"Thanks. Keep that smile on your face. It looks good on you."

He winks and walks toward the nurses' station.

Hoping Preston isn't in the break room, too, I take a deep breath and push open the door. Rebekah sits at the table, eating her breakfast sandwich.

"How can you eat that crap and not weigh five hundred pounds?" I tease her.

She shrugs and takes a huge bite. "God blessed me with a metabolism that runs non-stop," she mumbles.

"If we could all be so lucky... Hey, I wanted to tell you that Cammy and Michelle really hit it off. Michelle just loved her. First thing this morning, she asked me when Cammy could come over again."

"Cammy loved her, too. She told me she was the sweetest, smartest, funniest little girl she's ever met."

The door opens and Preston walks in, putting his lunch into the refrigerator. "Good morning, ladies," he says and walks out the door.

Rebekah looks at me, eyes narrowed. "You okay? You look like you're about ready to vomit."

"I'm fine. The door opening just startled me."

"Mmm-hmm..." She leans back in the chair. "What aren't you telling me?"

"I'm fine. Listen, I'll talk to you later. I need to put my stuff in the office before my first appointment gets here." I turn, hearing the chair scrape across the floor.

"Jayna, wait." She lowers her voice. "Is Dr. Joseph coming on to you?"

I swallow. "I really don't want to talk about it here." My mind is racing. Oh my god, he's done this to someone else. I just know it.

"I'm here if you ever want to talk."

I nod and head to my office. When I open the door and see Preston standing there, I jump. "You scared the crap out of me. What the hell are you doing in my office?"

"I didn't mean to scare you. I need to talk to you in private."

"Well, I don't have anything to say to you. I said all I wanted to say last night. So, unless this concerns a patient, please leave."

"Jayna, don't be that way. Couples have disagreements all the time. We'll get through this."

I throw my hands into the air. "Do you *hear* yourself? We are *not* a couple. I'm not going to ask you again before I call security. Please, leave my office."

"I'll give you time to think about everything. I love you." He turns and walks out.

My stomach roils, a shudder racking my body. My first instinct is to call Mitch, but he is probably busy. I take a deep breath. I can do this. I'm not going to let some unhinged man weaken me.

I sit behind my desk and look up the extension for HR before I change my mind.

"Human Resources, this is Lauren. How may I help you?"

"Hi, Lauren. This is Dr. Shipman at the Hartford Tower clinic. I have a few questions I hope you can help me with."

"Absolutely. I'll be happy to answer your questions or direct you to somebody who can."

"Thank you. What do I do if I'm having an issue with a co-worker being...inappropriate?"

"You can file a formal complaint now or, if you are worried about this person's reaction, begin compiling a log of behaviors. But if you feel unsafe, I urge you to make a formal complaint."

"Okay, that's what I thought. You were a big help. Thank you." I hang up, feeling better now that I know my next steps.

Preston stays away from me for the rest of the day. Mitch sent me a text earlier telling me he wasn't able to work on the paperwork because he had meetings all day. I told him not to worry about it, to get to it when he has time. Maybe Preston got the message this morning and will back off.

CHAPTER 19

~Mitch~

I can't believe Bronson made such a mess out of his case that I have to try and straighten everything out. That wasn't on my to-do list for today. I feel horrible that I couldn't get the sexual harassment paperwork completed for Jayna. I send her a text.

I'm sorry, but I have been slammed at work today and haven't been able to work on the paperwork for you yet. I will get it done as soon as I can.

It's okay. I know how busy you are and don't expect you to neglect your work. Preston was a little creepy this morning, but he hasn't talked to me since.

I don't trust him, Jayna. Have you called HR yet? Keep records of everything he does that makes you uncomfortable so we have a record of it.

Yes, I did. Thank you, Mitch. Have a good evening :)

It really shouldn't feel so good to talk to her, but it does. Time to call Luke and make plans to go out tonight. I can't let myself fall again. It will only bring pain.

Luke answers on the first ring. "Hey, man. I was just about to call you. Do you want to go to Big D's tonight?"

"That's actually why I was calling. I need to go out tonight. Plus, I want to thank you for all your help with the Taylor case. You were my ace in the hole, you kinky bastard," I chuckle.

"What are friends for? Let's just hope I can find me another woman as kinky as Zee. She checked all the boxes, except for the whole cheating thing. That's just not cool. What time do you want to meet, or do you want to ride together?"

"Let's meet there around nine. I don't want to ride together in case we get lucky."

"Good thinking, my man. I'll see you soon."

* * *

Since it's ladies' night, Big D's is hopping, beautiful women everywhere. Knowing only male bartenders work on ladies' night works out well. I didn't need to run into Molly again. Making my way to the bar, I scan the room, looking for Luke.

"What can I get you to drink, Mitch?"

"Hey, Bret. What are you doing tending bar tonight?"

"Josh called out, so that leaves me to help keep the ladies happy." He glances around and laughs. "No hardship here."

"Right you are. I'll take an Angry Orchard on tap."

"Coming right up."

A hard slap on my back about knocks me off my stool. I glance around to see Luke standing there, a huge smile on his face.

"Shit, man." I stretch out my shoulders. "That hurt. What the hell?"

"Don't be a pussy. I didn't hit you that hard. Did you order me a drink?"

Bret sets my drink down in front of me and smiles, hearing our banter.

"Order your own. I didn't know what you'd want or when you'd be here."

"We said nine." He looks at his watch. "It's only nine twenty. What are you drinking?"

"Angry Orchard on tap. This shit is delicious."

"Gag. I can't stand that shit. Give me a Heineken." As Bret walks away, Luke leans back against the bar, looking around the room. "So, have you scoped out any prospects yet?"

"Nope. I've only been here a few minutes myself."

"Any sign of the crazy bartender from a few weeks ago?"

"Only male bartenders work on ladies' night."

"I wondered what you were going to do if she was working." He laughs. "She'd probably put poison in your drinks."

"I wouldn't put that past her. Did I tell you I saw her last night when I was having dinner with Jayna and Dad?"

"Oh, man. How'd that go?"

I snort. "Awkward. Very, very awkward."

Luke bumps his shoulder against mine. "Look over there." He nods at the dance floor where there are a couple ladies bumping and grinding to the beat of the music. "I think it's time to work my way onto the dance floor. You in?"

I down my drink and slam the glass onto the bar. "Let's go."

I walk onto the dance floor and place my hands on the silver-blonde's hips, leaning down to whisper into her ear. "Have you been waiting on me?"

She tilts her head back, grinding her ass against my dick. "All my life, hot stuff."

We have fun on the dance floor, but it doesn't have the appeal it used to. I keep picturing dark hair, green eyes, and curves in all the right places.

When the woman nibbles on my ear, which is normally a sure way to turn me on, I feel nothing, not even a twitch.

She whispers, "Do you wanna get out of here?"

I close my eyes and take a deep breath. "Please don't take this the wrong way. You are beautiful, but I'm just not in the right frame of mind tonight."

"I understand, Mitch." She smiles. "I had fun dancing with you."

"Thanks."

I wave to Luke, getting his attention, then point to the door to let him know I'm leaving. He whispers something to the girl he's dancing with, then rushes over to me.

"Why are you leaving? We just got here."

"I'm just not feeling it. The only person I really want to be with is out of my league, yet still resides in my stone-cold heart."

"I think you need to have faith in yourself and let that cold heart thaw."

"Not sure if it's possible."

I give him a bro hug, then work my way through the crowd and out the door. Walking the two blocks to my car, I decide to go for a drive to clear my head. I find myself driving toward Jayna's high-rise, wondering if she's thinking about me like I am about her.

I pull over and grab my phone to text her.

What are you doing?

Watching a rerun of This Is Us. *You?*

Heading home from having drinks with Luke.

It's early. You're already calling it a night? :o

:) I just wasn't feeling it tonight.

What I really want to say is she's all I can think about, but I'm the last thing she needs in her life. My phone buzzes.

I have some leftover pizza if you're interested. Have you eaten?

No. I was going to grab a bite to eat at the bar, but left before I ordered anything. You know how much I love pizza.

*You've never been able to say no to pizza :) How long will it take you
to get here?*

Would it freak you out if I told you I was already here?

Ha-ha! Not at all. I'll let the doorman know to let you up.

See you in a second.

I rush across the street. When I get to the door, the doorman opens it, greeting me by name. "Hi, Mr. Davis. Dr. Shipman is expecting you."

"Thank you..." I glance down at his name badge, "Ralph. Have a nice evening."

"You, too, Mr. Davis."

I feel as anxious as I did years ago when I'd go see Jayna at her house. The elevator seems to take forever.

When the doors open, I see her standing in her doorway, holding a piece of pizza in her hand. She looks stunning with no make-up, her hair in a messy bun, wearing boxers and a baggy tank top. This is the Jayna I fell in love with so many years ago. Simple, beautiful, loving.

"You look delicious... I mean, *that* looks delicious." I wink and smile, her giggle music to my ears.

"Always the charmer, aren't you?"

"That's me."

"Come on in."

We walk into the living room, the pizza and a couple bottles of beer sitting on the coffee table. She gestures to the couch. "Have a seat. Michelle is asleep, but she sleeps like the dead, so you don't have to worry about whispering. She's going to be mad when she finds out you came over and she didn't get to see you."

"She's a great kid, Jayna. I always knew you'd be a wonderful mother. It shows in her sweet disposition."

Jayna takes a seat next to me on the couch. "Thank you. It's been hard. I never dreamed I'd be a single mother. Honestly, all I ever dreamed about was being a parent with you by my side. I guess life had other plans." Sadness is evident on her features, but she tries to cover it with a smile. "But she is the best gift I've ever received, so I'll never complain."

"Can I be honest with you?"

"I always want you to be honest with me, Mitch."

I place my elbows on my knees and hang my head, not daring to look at her. "It kills me that Michelle is not mine. That I pushed you away thinking it was for your own good. When Mom died, I just lost myself. I didn't let others see how dark things got for me, but you knew. I'm so sorry I took it out on you when you called after she passed. I was so mad, Jayna, but not at you. At myself. At the world. Dad was a complete mess after losing his best friend. His world. At that moment, I knew I'd never make it if what happened to them happened to us, so I pushed you away and made you think I hated you for not calling sooner. I regret that more than you'll ever know."

"Mitch," Jayna whispers and takes my hand, urging me to look into her emerald eyes that shine with tears. "Not once have I ever hated you or stopped wishing for you to come back to me. I know we aren't the same people we were all those years ago, but how about we start by being friends again and see what happens."

I smile, squeezing her hand. "I'd like that. What about Michelle's father? What kind of man leaves his child?"

She sighs. "Her father was one of the residents at the hospital. I thought I might be able to fall in love with him. We were both driven and seemed to have so much in common. Turned out we really had nothing in common. Medical school was a means to an end for him. He comes from a wealthy family who told him he had to become a doctor, then join Doctors Without Borders in order to get his sizable inheritance. When I told him I was pregnant, he told me to 'take care of it'. Like the child I was carrying wasn't even a life. He was adamant that a baby wasn't part of his plans. So I basically told him to fuck off. I did call him the day she was born, and he told me not to list him on her birth certificate. I was all too happy to oblige."

With every word she speaks, I get more angry. "What a selfish bastard. He's not a father. He's a sperm donor. I'm so sorry. I feel like this is all my fault."

"It's not your fault. We can't dwell on the past, Mitch. It's done. I'll make sure she never wants for anything. I'll be both a mom and a dad to her."

I shake my head in awe. "You are amazing, Jayna. I'm sorry I made you relive all of that." I'm such an idiot, the lawyer in me coming out with an inquisition.

She slaps my arm lightly. "I just do what any good mother would."

She picks up the tv remote. "Enough of this talk. Do you want to watch something?"

"Do you remember when we would binge watch *The Big Bang Theory*?"

She laughs. "Yes. We practically knew the words to every single episode. It drove our parents crazy. Do you want me to see if I can find it?"

A grin takes over my face. "Sounds like old times."

* * *

I open my eyes to see a miniature version of Jayna staring at me. "Hi, Mr. Mitch. Why are you and Mommy asleep on the couch?"

Shit. I glance down to see Jayna asleep, her head in my lap.

"Good morning, Michelle," I whisper. "I came over to visit last night. I guess your mommy and I fell asleep watching tv."

"Okay. Can I have a Pop-Tart?"

Jayna stirs in my lap, then suddenly sits up, pushing hair out of her face as she stares at Michelle. "Oh... Hi, sweetheart. Mr. Mitch—"

"I know, Mommy. Mr. Mitch told me he came over to visit and you two fell asleep watching tv. I'm sad I didn't get to watch tv with Mr. Mitch, too."

I sit up and tickle her side. "I'll come over again and we can all watch tv together. You can even pick what you want to watch."

"Really?" Her face lights up. "Did you hear that, Mommy? He's going to come over again and watch tv with me, too. Can I have a Pop-Tart?"

"You know those aren't good for you. How about scrambled eggs and toast?" She turns to me. "Mitch, would you like some eggs and toast?"

"I don't want to put you out. It's so early."

"I'm fixing them anyway. And this is Michelle's standard time. She wakes up at six thirty every day."

"Then eggs are a good choice, because she is up with the chickens," I joke.

Michelle looks around the room, brows furrowed. "I don't see any chickens. Where are the chickens?"

"Baby, Mr. Mitch was just teasing. *Up with the chickens* means it's way too early to wake up."

Placing her hands on her hips, she scrunches up her nose. "That's just silly, Mr. Mitch."

This kid is just too damn cute. "I know. I'm silly.

"I like you, silly Mitch. Will you read me a story while Mommy makes us breakfast?"

"I'd love to. Go and pick a book."

Jayna laughs and stands as Michelle runs to her room and grabs what looks to be every book she can carry. "Here you go, Mr. Mitch. These are all my favoritests."

"Hop up," I say, patting my lap, "I bet we have time for one or two."

In no time, Jayna whips up scrambled eggs. "Almost ready."

Michelle jumps up and grabs my hand, pulling me to the kitchen.

"It smells delicious." I didn't realize how hungry I was until my stomach let out a loud growl.

"Did you hear that, Mommy? Mr. Mitch's stomach talked to us. It said, 'Feed me some eggs'." She jumps up and down at the counter. "Can I push down the toast? Mr. Mitch, will you pick me up so I can reach?"

I look at Jayna, who nods with a smile. "Of course. You are such a good helper. I bet this is going to be the best toast I've ever had."

"Mommy makes cinnamon butter that is so yummy on the toast. You have ta try it."

"If you say it's good, then I will."

Michelle and I take a seat at the breakfast bar while Jayna waits for the toast to finish.

Jayna plates the toast and places it in front of us. I take a piece, making a production of spreading the butter all over it, then take a big bite. "Yum. You're right, Michelle. This is the best toast I've ever eaten."

Michelle jumps off her stool and starts dancing around, throwing her arms in the air in victory.

"Sit down and eat your breakfast, lil' lady, before it gets cold," Jayna mock scolds her.

"I'm sorry, Momma." She climbs back up on the stool.

Breakfast is delicious, but the company is even better.

"I'm all done. May I please be excused?" Michelle asks politely.

Jayna nods, and Michelle jumps down.

"Can I help you wash the dishes, Jayna?"

"No. There are only a few. I'm just going to put them in the dishwasher."

Michelle pulls on my hand. "Dance with me, please."

"How can I say no to the cutest girl in the world?" I take her hand and twirl her in circles all the way into the living room. We both giggle and crash onto the couch to read one last book.

I look over and see Jayna leaning against the breakfast bar, smiling. She catches me looking and walks into the living room, sitting next to us and pulling Michelle into a hug.

I could stay here all day, but duty calls. "I wish I didn't have to go, but I need to run home and get ready for court."

Jayna nods. "We need to get ready, too. Michelle, go brush your teeth, then get dressed. I put your clothes on your beanbag chair."

"Okay, Mommy." Michelle pulls away from Jayna's embrace, jumps into my arms, and kisses my cheek. "Bye, Mr. Mitch. I hope you come back soon." She leans in and gives me a hug before taking off down the hallway toward her bedroom.

"See you soon, lil' lady," I yell as she vanishes down the hall.

I smile at Jayna. "I had a wonderful time last night. I'm sorry I fell asleep and Michelle found me here this morning."

"You have nothing to be sorry for. I had a wonderful time, too. I hope we can do it again sometime soon."

I pull her into a hug and place a gentle kiss on her soft lips. "Me, too, Jayna. Me, too." I can feel the wall around my heart start to crumble a little more. "I'll talk to you soon."

CHAPTER 20

~Jayna~

It's been two weeks since Mitch kissed me, but I can still feel it on my lips. With each conversation we have, I see more and more of the old Mitch coming through. It's like things are starting to fall into place.

I've noticed Preston looking my way occasionally, but he hasn't made any inappropriate remarks or tried to pressure me into going out with him. I told Mitch to hold off on the sexual harassment paperwork for now. I've contacted HR, and if he does anything else, I'll make a formal complaint.

A grin spreads across my face when I get a text from Mitch that only contains several pizza emojis.

Ha-ha... Are you trying to tell me you're hungry, or did the pizza emoji get stuck?

I'm always hungry. But what I was trying to do is ask you if you and Michelle would like to go get pizza tonight?

That sounds like fun. I know Michelle will be thrilled to see you. She asks about you several times a day and looks inside Starbucks every morning to see if you're in there. You picked a good day to get dinner. Mom and Dad are coming in tomorrow to pick her up for a week while the weather is still nice in Ohio.

Awww... That's wonderful that your parents make the effort to spend so much time with her. She's a lucky little girl.

She's spoiled :D

There is no such thing as too spoiled when it comes to grandchildren. Or so I hear. BTW, sorry I've been so busy. They fired one of the associates, so until we hire someone new, my workload has increased. We had several interviews this morning with a few promising prospects, so things should settle down pretty quickly.

That's good, Mr. Junior Partner.

It still seems so unreal :o

I always knew you would be the best lawyer out there.

You always did have too much faith in me.

Never. What time do you want to pick us up?

How does six sound? Does that give you enough time?

That sounds great. It's my Friday to only work half a day, so I'm going to the grocery store, then picking up Michelle around three.

I'm looking forward to seeing you both.

Me, too.

I wonder if I have a goofy grin on my face. I should've known I wasn't truly in love with Doug, because he never once made me feel like Mitch does just from a simple text conversation.

* * *

It's so hard to keep a secret from Michelle, but I want to surprise her. Since we got home, she's told me several times that she's ready to eat and wants to know what I'm cooking.

"Mommy, I'm hungry."

I'm saved by the doorbell.

Michelle looks at me. "Can I get it?"

"Yes, but you need to ask who it is first."

She runs to the door. "Who is it?" she yells.

"It's Mr. Mitch."

Her eyes go wide, her face full of excitement when she looks at me. "It's Mr. Mitch, Mommy. Can he come in?"

"Of course. Open the door."

Michelle gets up on her tiptoes and pulls down on the lever, pulling open the door. "Mr. Mitch! You came back to see me. I've missed you."

He kneels, and Michelle throws her arms around his neck. "I've missed you, too, sweet girl. I thought I'd see if you and your mommy want to get some pizza and play some arcade games."

"Wow, Michelle. Doesn't that sound like fun?"

"Yes! I love pizza."

"Let me grab your car seat, then we can go. Will her seat fit in the back of your car, Mitch?"

He laughs. "Yes, but that's about all it can hold."

It takes me a few minutes to get the car seat into his car. When I turn around, I fight back tears seeing Mitch and Michelle together. She sits on his shoulders, giggling as he gallops on the sidewalk. It gives me a glimpse at what a wonderful father Mitch would be. Longing hits me.

"All ready. Mommy finally got it in this fancy car," I tease.

"For such a little thing, you sure need a lot of room, Michelle."

"You need a minivan like Mimi so you have room for all my stuff when we go places," Michelle says innocently, not knowing how much I wish he had a reason to have a bigger car.

Mitch takes Michelle off of his shoulders, placing her into her car seat and buckling her in.

"Mr. Mitch would look silly driving a minivan," he says as he tightens the straps on her harness.

I think he would look sexy as hell driving a minivan. He will probably be the star of my dreams tonight, doing dirty things to me in a minivan. Not paying attention, I almost shut my foot in the door. I need to snap out of it.

Mitch climbs into the car, his sexy cologne surrounding me. Just like that, the dirty thoughts are back.

"You looked like an old pro buckling Michelle in."

"I've done my fair share of getting Emily into and out of her car seat."

"Such a good big brother," I tease.

Michelle talks non-stop as we drive to the pizzeria.

We look like the perfect family walking into the restaurant, both Mitch and I holding one of Michelle's hands. Her eyes widen at all the games and flashing lights.

Mitch is a trooper as Michelle pulls him to all the different games. Luckily, she doesn't care if she's playing the game or not. She just likes pushing the buttons.

Once we sit, the waitress comes to the table. "Your little girl is so cute. She looks like a daddy's girl."

Mitch smiles. For once, my little peanut keeps her mouth shut.

"Thank you," I say, leaving it at that.

After we order and she walks away, I lean toward Mitch. "I'm sorry. I should have corrected her."

"It's nobody's business."

When our pizza arrives, we all dig in, making small talk and laughing. It is delicious, and I eat way too much.

"Thank you for this, Mitch."

"It was the perfect release after a long, stressful week at work."

We stand to leave. Michelle yawns and reaches up for Mitch to pick her up. He carries her to the car, my heart swelling when she lays her head on his shoulder and closes her eyes. He carefully places her into the car seat and buckles her in.

Michelle is asleep before we make it out of the parking lot.

When we get home, Mitch carries her inside. "Where do you want me to put her?"

"We can put her in bed. She went to the bathroom before we left the pizzeria, so she should be good."

Mitch carries her to her room, gently placing her onto her bed. "Good night, sweet girl," he softly whispers as he places a kiss on the top of her head. I swallow the emotion from seeing his loving gesture, quickly wiping the tears that fall from my eyes before he joins me in the hallway.

I take a deep breath. "Would you like a cold beer?"

"That sounds great."

I grab us each a beer and carry them to the living room. I kick off my shoes and curl up on the couch.

Mitch follows suit, sitting down next to me. He leans back, placing his arms on the back of the couch, as if he does this every day. Turning to me, he asks, "How are things at work. Is Dr. Douche staying professional?"

"I've felt like he was watching me a few times, but he hasn't sent any texts or cornered me in the office."

Mitch places his hand on my thigh. "I will do anything to keep you safe. You have to tell me if he crosses the line again. I will make sure it's the last time."

"You've always been protective of me."

Mitch reaches up and runs his finger down my cheek, causing me to suck in a breath. "That's what I'm supposed to do."

We are drawn together slowly, like two moths to a flame. Our lips crash together with unstoppable passion and desire that's been building since the minute we saw each other again.

Mitch pulls back, panting. "Is this okay?"

"God yes. I need you like I need air to breathe."

That is all the permission he needs. He slowly pushes me back onto the couch, covering my body with his. Heat pools between my legs, making me rub against him to soothe the ache.

"I can feel your arousal, Jayna. God, I've missed you. Let me make you feel good."

"Yes, please...

Heaven is too small a word to describe how I feel as his fingers trail up my thigh and into the leg of my shorts, under my lace thong, and into my wet heat. It's been so long since I've been touched by a man, I almost come immediately. Mitch nips and sucks on my lips and neck as he plunges two fingers into me. He covers my mouth with his right as I explode, swallowing my screams.

After a few minutes, he pulls back, smiling. "That was even more beautiful than I remember."

"That was even more *amazing* than I remember. It's your turn. Let *me* make *you* feel good."

"No," he peppers kisses up my neck and to my mouth. "This...*kiss*...was...*kiss*...just...*kiss*...for...*kiss*...you...*kiss*." He pulls his fingers out of me and licks them, moaning. "You taste like heaven."

Mitch rolls off of me, pulling my back flush to his front, holding me tightly. "I don't want to just be friends, Jayna. I want to be more. I need you back in my life. Do you think you'll ever be able to forgive me for pushing you away and being such a jerk?"

I twist around to face him. "That's all I've ever wanted. I've never forgotten the words you said to me when I left for Harvard."

"I haven't, either. '*I love you. Go. Become the best damn doctor the world has ever seen. We'll always find our way back to each other.*' And that's exactly what we did. I won't let anything come between us again. We've both worked so hard to get where we are right now. We just have to learn to trust each other again."

"I want that more than anything, Mitch. I won't lie and say I'm not scared. It may take me a while to feel secure, but I want us."

"I promise to spend the rest of my days making it up to you. All the women who came after meant nothing to me. Not one could erase you from my mind, no matter how hard I tried. I hate that my past may pop up unexpectedly...like you witnessed at the restaurant. I'm not proud of that, Jayna. But what I can promise is you are the only woman I will ever want."

CHAPTER 21

~Mitch~

It was so hard to leave Jayna last night, but we need to take things slow. I couldn't have Michelle walking in on me ravishing her mother on the couch. She will soon be with her grandparents for a week, so Jayna and I will have plenty of time to reconnect and find each other again. She promised to call me this afternoon after her parents take Michelle back to Ohio.

Dad is going to be ecstatic when I tell him Jayna and I are going to give our relationship another chance. Henry will be elated, too. Elated that he can say *I told you so.*

I pick up the phone and give my dad a call. The phone rings several times before his voicemail picks up. I hang up without leaving a message. He'll call me back. Then I push my brother's contact number. Henry picks up after the first ring.

"Hey, bro. I see I'm your second choice."

I frown. "What are you talking about?"

"Dad's on the ladder, painting the trim. We couldn't get to his phone before it went to voicemail. Then my phone rings." He chuckles. "I see how it is."

"Don't be a tit. Put me on speaker so I can share my news with everybody. Are the girls there, too?"

I hear both Kristi and Marley say, "Hi, Mitch."

"Hi, y'all. I have some good news."

Kristi pipes in first. "Ooo, do tell. I hope this news has to do with a certain dark-haired beauty."

"Actually, it does. After Jayna and I ran into each other a little over a month ago, all those old feelings came crashing back. As hard as I tried to fight it, my heart wants what it wants. She is even more amazing than she was all those years ago, and her little girl is absolutely precious. She's so smart and looks just like her mommy. I fell in love with her the moment we met. Jayna has agreed to give us another chance, and I'm going to do everything I can to be the man you raised me to be, Dad."

I can hear sniffing in the background and know it's the girls.

"I'm so happy for you, son. After I saw you two together, I had no doubt it would only be a matter of time before you found yourself again."

"I'm proud of you, too, bro. Welcome to the love club." Henry laughs.

Marley speaks up next. "Your mother loved her so much. I know she is happy as can be right now. I hope you'll bring her and her daughter with you when you come back for Emily's dance recital."

"That's my plan. Emily and Michelle will love each other."

"Don't fuck it up, bro." I hear a slap. "Ouch. You didn't have to hit me so hard." I hear a sigh. "I'll put a dollar in the swear jar."

Kristi laughs. "Thanks, Mitch. You just gained me another dollar. At this rate, I'll be able to afford to take off for twelve *months* after the baby is born instead of twelve weeks. Henry can't seem to keep his swearing to a minimum. The baby's first word will probably be shit, damn, or hell."

I laugh. "Good luck with that. Goodbye, everyone. I'll see you in a couple of weeks."

* * *

I call Luke and see if he wants to meet at the gym. I'm overdue for a workout. Besides, I need to make sure the employees are still doing what Dad asked them to do.

"Hey, man. Do you want to get your sweat on?"

I hear him groan. "Fighting a hangover. You sure missed a good time at Big D's last night. The women were wild and crazy. Your not so favorite bartender was there, so it was probably a good thing you weren't. If the way she glared at me was any indication of how she feels about you, she's one woman scorned."

"I seriously think she is crazy. Anyway, I'm not interested in her or any other woman at that bar."

"The *fuck?* You, not interested in a warm, willing woman? Are you sick?"

I chuckle. "No, man. I'm better than I've been for the first time in years. Jayna is back in my life, and for the first time in a long time, everything feels right."

"Just like that? I've never met Jayna, but her pus—"

"Don't you fucking *dare* finish that sentence. She is my everything. Always has been. I've just been too afraid to acknowledge how much I needed and missed her."

"Sorry, man. I had no idea. If you're happy, I'm happy. What time do you want to meet up? I'll need to grab a quick shower to rejuvenate myself and wash off the smell of last night."

"Gross. You should've washed that shit off when you got home. I'll meet you there in thirty."

"Sounds good. See you there."

* * *

When I pull up at the gym, I hear Luke before I see him. As always, he sits in his truck jamming out to Hank, Jr. I slap my hand on his window, startling him. He rolls down the window. "You going to sit out here all day, or are we going to go in and hit the iron?"

"I was just waitin' on you, jackass."

We grab our bags. The second we walk in, I hear, "Hi, Mr. Davis. How are you today?"

I want to say *stop kissing my ass,* but I don't. "Hi, Gretta, Neal. How's it going?"

Neal, the gym's manager, smiles. "Things are going great. I've implemented the no cell phone incentive, and a lot of our members embrace it. There seems to be less sitting on the equipment and more working out."

"That's great. I'll be sure and pass that along to my dad."

I turn away and see Luke checking out Tabitha wiping down the equipment. She looks up and smiles at him. I shake my head. He needs to just go for it and ask her out.

"She just smiled at you," I say, nudging him with my shoulder. "You should go talk to her. You know you want to."

"She's working, man. If she wants to talk, she can come find me."

We try to hit every piece of equipment in the gym, Luke lifting more or going faster than usual, showing off in front of Tabitha.

Sweat dripping down my nose, I stand from the row machine and turn to Luke, wiping off my face. "I'm done. We've been at it for over an hour. I'm expecting a call from Jayna and don't want to miss it. Call you later."

"You've got it bad, man. It's strange seeing you actually care about a woman. Ever since I've known you, you've been Mr. One And Done."

"Well, get used to it, because I don't plan on her going anywhere." I pick up my phone from the desk and head to the car.

* * *

I clean the house in the hopes Jayna will agree to come over tonight and let me cook her dinner.

My phone rings. Seeing Jayna's name on my screen, I smile as I answer. "Hello, beautiful. How did you know I was thinking about you?"

She laughs. "Probably because we share the same brainwaves. I just dropped Michelle and my parents off at the airport. She was so excited. I couldn't believe they flew in this morning and booked their return flight for this afternoon."

"I'm not going to complain. I was actually hoping to convince you to come over to my place for dinner tonight."

"You're cooking me dinner? Since when do you know how to cook?"

I chuckle. "I had to either learn to cook or live on takeout. You can only eat out so long before you get burned out."

"True. I would love to come over and taste your culinary skills firsthand."

"That sounds so dirty," I tease.

"Your mind is always in the gutter, Mitch. Some things never change. What time do you want me to come over?"

"I'll send an Uber for you around six. Does that give you enough time?"

"It's four now." She snorts. "I *hope* I can be presentable in two hours."

"You would be presentable in a paper sack. You don't have to get all dressed up. I just want to spend time with you."

"Better watch out. I could get used to hearing you talk like that. I've missed you."

I let out a sigh. "I've been a miserable man to deal with for a lot of years. The minute I saw you again, my heart slowly started thawing. Like I said, I was a fool and hate that you saw it up close and personal."

"Only you have the power to make sure that never happens again."

"I can't wait to see you, Jayna. I'd better start working my magic in the kitchen."

She chuckles. "I can't wait. See you soon."

I hang up and get busy, placing the potatoes into the oven and chopping the veggies to put on the kabobs with the steak I already have marinating in the refrigerator. I did cheat and picked up a few slices of lemon loaf from Starbucks this morning for dessert. I have whipped cream and fresh strawberries for an added touch.

The time flies by, and just as I finish cleaning up the kitchen, the doorbell rings. My heart rate increases as I open the door and see Jayna standing there in her white, strapless sundress, her black curls cascading over her bare shoulders and down her back.

"My god, you're a vision. Please, come in."

Jayna takes in my home with a look of appreciation on her face. "Your place is so nice, Mitch. It fits you. These floors are gorgeous."

"Thanks. I picked them out myself. I love the look of weathered wood tile."

She makes her way across my living room. "Your view out of these floor-to-ceiling windows is incredible. You can see the entire downtown from here."

"You standing in front of it makes it even more stunning."

Jayna smiles brightly. "You're making me blush, Mitch."

"Then I'm doing my job. You should always feel beautiful and desired." I clear my voice, gesturing to the kitchen. "Are you hungry? Dinner is ready."

"Yes, it smells wonderful. What did you fix?"

"I grilled kabobs and made twice-baked potatoes. Sound good?"

"That sounds delicious." She licks her lips, causing my dick to twitch.

Down boy. There will be time for that later.

"I also have your favorite for dessert."

Her eyes widen. "Lemon loaf?"

"What else?"

"You remember everything."

"I've forgotten nothing about you, Jayna."

"Me, either. You're a hard man to forget."

"Come on. Let's go into the dining room. I have some champagne chilling."

I lead her into the dining room that opens to both the kitchen and living area. The flickering candles make her look even more angelic.

"Have a seat," I say, pulling out her chair. "I'm going to go get the food."

"Thank you. This is all so beautiful."

I walk back in and set down the plates. "Thank you for coming over. I hope it tastes good."

"If it tastes anything like it looks and smells, then it will be amazing." She takes a mouthful of steak and moans out her appreciation.

I groan. "Woman, you are killing me here!"

"What do you mean?" she asks coyly, licking her lips and taking another bite.

She continues to torture me throughout the meal.

Finally, Jayna groans and pushes away her empty plate. "I'm stuffed. I couldn't eat another bite."

Smiling, I scoop her up and carry her to the couch. "Since you don't want dessert right now, we'll save it for later."

Jayna pats her stomach. "Give me some time and I'll be ready."

"We have all the time in the world. What do you want to do now?"

"Can we snuggle on the couch and listen to music?"

I pick up the remote to my sound system and turn it on. Brett Young's "In Case You Didn't Know" comes through the speakers. I pull her close and whisper, "In case you didn't know, I'm crazy about you. I'll spend the rest of my life proving just how much."

She sighs. "It's not just me now, Mitch. Michelle and I are a package deal."

"I know that, baby. All I see is you when I look at her. I will love her as if she were my own. She is one amazing little girl."

She climbs onto my lap and gives me a passionate kiss, which I enthusiastically return. "I need you," she pants. "It's been so long since I've felt you everywhere. Please, make love to me, Mitch."

"You don't know how badly I've wanted to hear those words. Are you sure you're ready? I'm content just to hold you in my arms again."

"I want this. I want you."

I scoop her up and carry her to my room. She will be the first woman I've had in my bed. I've taken all the others to the guest room. My room has always been my private space, but I want Jayna in my space more than I want my next breath.

Lowering her to the bed, I skim my hands down her sides, unzipping the side zipper on her dress as I go. I suck in a breath when her glorious, full breasts are on display, her hard nipples ready for me to devour. I pull off her dress and drop it to the floor, then kiss my way up her legs, swirling my tongue around her navel and trailing it up to her breasts. She lets out a moan when I suck one pink bud into my mouth.

"Mmmm. God, I've missed you...this...us." I turn my attention to her other breast before making my way to the white lace that's barely covering her pussy. I blow on her, making her shudder.

"I need your mouth on me, Mitch. Please."

"Where, baby?"

"My pussy. I'm dying to feel your tongue on me."

I smile. "Your wish is my command." I tear the small scrap of fabric from her body and eat her like it's my last meal.

She starts panting, her thighs quivering, then screams out my name and pulses around my tongue.

I crawl up her body, the evidence of her desire on my lips. She pulls me down and kisses me. "I taste delicious on you."

"Baby, you're the most delectable thing on earth."

My dick twitches, begging to be released. I'm afraid I'll explode with just one touch. I need to get myself under control or this will be over before it even begins.

"I want your cock inside me. I can feel how badly you want me."

I stand and pull down my jeans and briefs, my cock almost sighing with relief at being released. Jayna's eyes grow wide as a slow smile spreads across her face.

"You're even more beautiful than I remember."

I slide on a condom and crawl onto her body. "Are you ready for me?"

"I've never been more ready."

Reaching down, I guide my cock through her slickness, then slide into her warmth. I can't stop the tears from forming in my eyes, matching the ones glistening in hers. "I'm home, baby. I'm home."

"Promise me you'll never leave me again," whispers Jayna.

"I'm yours forever."

CHAPTER 22

~Jayna~

Last week was the best of my life. That first dinner at Mitch's was the first of many. Things are really starting to fall into place for us. We spent every spare minute together, learning everything that has happened to both of us over the years. We also spent a hell of a lot of time reacquainting ourselves with each other's bodies. That man certainly knows what he's doing. He is magical in the bedroom.

Michelle and I Facetimed every day. She got so excited each time I called her while Mitch was with me. My parents asked if she could stay another week, to which I agreed. Mitch and I will fly to Ohio to get her, then fly to Arkansas for Emily's dance recital. He asked if we could visit his mother's grave while we were there. It's been too hard for him to go alone. Having me by his side will make it easier. I had gone to her grave not long after I found out I was pregnant with Michelle and broke down, telling her how sorry I was and how much I wished Mitch were the father.

My phone rings, startling me out of my thoughts. Looking at the caller ID, my stomach drops.

I sigh. "What do you want, Preston?"

"Is that any way to talk to me? I think I've been quite understanding and have let you have your *fun*, but it's time you realize that you are mine. You coming here was destiny, an answer to my prayers."

"You're out of your mind. If there's any destiny to be had, it was that I met up with Mitch again. *He* is my destiny. If you don't stop contacting me, you'll leave me no choice but to file harassment charges against you."

"I wouldn't do that if I were you," he growls. "You don't know who you are toying with."

"I'm not *toying* with anybody. I didn't give you any reason to think I was interested in you. We danced one time at a club. I have told you repeatedly that I'm not interested in you."

Before he can respond, I hang up.

With shaky hands, I call Mitch. I'm crying uncontrollably when he answers.

"Hi, bab—" His voice turns from flirty to frantic when he hears me. "What's wrong, Jayna? What happened?"

"Oh, Mitch... I thought Preston was over his infatuation with me. It's been weeks since he's been inappropriate. He just called, telling me he's let me have my fun, but I'm his. I was sent here for him. He's freaking psychotic."

"I'm going to kill that *motherfucker*! What in the hell is wrong with him? I'm on my way over. We're going to document this and include it with what we already have. I'll file harassment charges tomorrow. You have tried to resolve this. Quite frankly, I'm pissed that HR didn't do anything. He's *threatened* you. Do you want me to come with you to speak with HR?"

"Yes, please. I swear, I've never encouraged him. I only danced with him that one time."

"Baby, you did nothing wrong. I was an ass when I inferred that you led him on. I wish I could go back and change so much of the past, but then you wouldn't have Michelle."

"Thank you."

"You never have to thank me for taking care of you. I'll be there shortly."

CHAPTER 23

~Mitch~

Having just filed the harassment paperwork, my anger simmers under the surface. I'll make sure Dr. Preston Joseph suffers the consequences of his behavior. Jayna and I were up late last night going over everything, her crying, me comforting her.

I haven't heard from her yet this morning, but she has to be ready for her second cup of coffee by now. I look at my watch, seeing it's almost noon. Maybe I can catch her on her lunch break and we can go speak to Charles, the HR manager, together. Maybe having a lawyer with her will make him realize just how serious this is.

"Margaret, I'm going out to lunch. I'm not sure when I'll be back. Call me if something comes up."

"No worries. I'll take care of whatever I can. Enjoy your lunch."

I try and keep my anger in check as the elevator descends to the second floor. I don't know what I'll do if I run into that prick.

When I get to the waiting room, it's empty, the *out to lunch* sign sitting on the receptionist's desk. I see Rebekah in the office, putting away a file.

She looks up and smiles brightly. "Hi, Mitch."

"Hi, Rebekah. Is Jayna here?"

"I think she's in her office. You can go on back. Second door on the right."

When I get to the door, it's slightly ajar. I poke my head in. Empty. I wonder if she's gone to lunch or is still with a patient. I'll leave her a note, telling her to call me. All I see are files on her desk, which is odd. Jayna was never one to leave her desk a mess. Searching for Post-it notes, not seeing any, I pull open the top drawer, my eyes narrowing. I can't believe my eyes when I see pictures of Jayna, some taken in her private bathroom. This isn't Jayna's desk. It's the creepy doctor's. He has cameras hidden in her office?! The word *MINE* is scrawled in red over all the pictures.

I'm going to kill him.

I grab my phone and quickly snap pictures of all the photos. I don't even bother to shut the drawer before I stride to the door, stopping in my tracks when I hear a muffled "stop" coming from across the hallway.

When I hear a scream, I burst through the door to see Jayna being pressed back against her desk, Preston lying on her with his hand over her mouth.

In a blind rage, I stride up to them and tear him away from her, slamming him into the wall. "Get your *fucking* hands off of her."

"Mitch, thank God."

I grab her and pull her close, feeling her trembling. "I've got you, baby. I'm going to make sure he never gets near you again." I turn to the wall, seeing Preston's gone. "That slimy *bastard*. We need to call the police and report this. This was assault."

"What if they don't believe me?"

"I'm a witness. Plus, once they see what I found in his office, there's no way he can get out of it."

"What did you find?" she questions, her voice shaking.

"Are you sure you want to see?"

"Yes..."

"Call the police, then I'll show you and them at the same time. I'm going to look for Preston."

Just as I walk out of Jayna's office, Rebekah comes rushing down the hallway. "What happened? Preston just tore out of the office, muttering. What the hell is going on?"

"So he left?"

"Yes. Now tell me what the *hell* just happened."

"You didn't hear anything?" I question in a tone harsher than it should be.

"No, I was making copies in the copy room. That damn copy machine is so loud you can't hear anything."

I clench my fists. "That *bastard* just attacked Jayna. I heard her scream and found him over the top of her, covering her mouth."

Rebekah's face morphs into utter shock and horror. "Is she okay? I knew he had a thing for her, but I had no idea he was so unhinged to do something like that. Did you call the police?"

"She is calling them right now."

We walk into Jayna's office. She's crying softly in her chair, her arms wrapped around herself. I feel so helpless. If I would've gotten here a few minutes earlier, maybe I could have prevented this.

I rush over to her, pulling her into my arms. "Shhh, baby. It's going to be okay. I'll make sure of it. Did he hurt you?"

"He slapped me and pulled me to my desk by my hair. Who knows what he would've done if you hadn't come in. Oh god, Mitch. I feel sick."

Rebekah comes around the desk and holds her arms out. Jayna cries harder when Rebekah pulls her into a hug. "Jayna, I'm so sorry I didn't hear you. I never dreamed Preston would really do something like this. He's always had a weird vibe about him, but I just thought that was him. *Shit.* I bet he's done this before. I wonder if that's why we have such a huge turnover of female staff."

I start pacing, needing to move. "I sure hope not. I going to dig into his background and see what I can find out. He won't know what hit him after I get through."

Rebekah squeezes Jayna's hand. "I'm going to call a couple of the on-call physicians to come in and cover the patients this afternoon. I doubt Preston will be back, and you need to talk to the cops, then go home."

"Thank you, Rebekah," Jayna and I say at the same time.

The bell chimes when the clinic door opens. "I bet that's the police." Rebekah rushes out. A few minutes later, she escorts two officers, one female and one male, into the office.

The female officer looks at Jayna, then me. "I'm Officer Nichols, and this is Officer Farris. Jayna Shipman?"

"Yes. I want to report an assault by one of the other doctors on staff."

The officer looks at me. "And who is this gentleman?"

"Mitch Davis, her boyfriend."

"I would like him to stay with me while I do this."

"Of course. We have some questions for you. Do you feel like answering them here, or would you rather come down to the police station?"

Jayna looks at me. "I'd like to get this over with as soon as possible."

She nods. "We can do it right here."

"Thank you. Also, Mitch said he found something disturbing just before finding me."

Officer Farris looks at Mitch. "What is it that you've found?"

"Let me show you."

I lead them down the hallway to his office. "This is the first time I've actually come back here to the private offices. I was coming to surprise Jayna and take her to lunch. I guess I misunderstood which office Rebekah said was Jayna's. When I realized she wasn't in here, I looked for something to write a note on. I opened the top desk drawer, shocked by what I found."

Officer Nichols turns to Jayna. "Whose office is this?"

"Dr. Preston Joseph's, the man who assaulted me."

Both officers look into the drawer, stunned. When Jayna sees, she gasps and starts shaking her head. "No, no, no. This can't be happening to me. Those are taken in the *bathroom* in my office. I'm going to be sick."

It takes everything in me to hold it together. I'm so angry. All I want to do is find that sick bastard and beat the shit out of him.

Officer Nichols takes notes, while Officer Farris takes pictures of the photos. We are just about to walk out of the office when Preston comes busting in with...

What the hell?

"Maxon? What are you doing here?" I ask.

"I could ask you the same thing, Mitch. Why are you in Preston's office?"

Preston's face is red with rage. "What the fuck, Dad? How do you know him?"

I furrow my brows. "*Dad?* I thought you just had daughters."

"I'm his *bastard* child he doesn't claim. He'd like to lock me away just like he did my mother," Preston seethes.

Maxon glares at him. "I think it would be best if you kept your mouth shut, Preston."

Officer Nichols looks at Preston. "Sir, do we have permission to search your office?"

He looks at Maxon, who shakes his head. "No, you don't."

Rebekah comes into the office, phone in her hand. "You don't need his permission. I have our HR manager on the line to speak with you." She hands over the phone.

Officer Nichols walks away, talks a few minutes, then nods to Officer Farris, who pulls out his cuffs and wrenches Preston's arms behind his back.

"You can't do this," Preston screams. "She is mine. I did nothing wrong. I just wanted to claim what is mine."

"*Be quiet!*" Maxon tells him. "I will meet you down at the station."

By this time, the other doctors and nurses have returned from lunch and patients have started checking in. The officers take Preston out the back entrance to keep the commotion to a minimum. I know there is no way the people in the waiting room didn't hear him screaming, though.

Maxon looks at me and growls, "We need to talk. *Now.*"

"Jayna, sweetheart, I need to speak with Maxon for a minute. Then I'll meet you in your office." I kiss her before she walks away, Rebekah's arm around her.

The minute they leave, Maxon snarls, "You need to make this go away. I don't care what it takes, but you *will* make that woman recant everything she has accused my son of. I've worked too hard to keep him out of the news."

I cross my arms, shaking my head. "I won't do that, Maxon. You of all people know it's not her choice now. The prosecutor's office is the one who presses charges. Jayna means everything to me. Not to mention I *saw* Preston assaulting her. I'm sorry, but your son has some serious issues he needs to take care of. I just filed harassment paperwork this morning. He took things too far, Maxon."

He steps closer. "If you want to remain a junior partner at the firm, I suggest you think this over very carefully." With that, he storms out of the clinic.

What the hell? I wonder if the rest of the partners know what is going on? Do they know he's been covering up for his son? Do they even know he has a son? I'll figure that out later. Right now, I just want to wrap Jayna in my arms and take all her pain away.

CHAPTER 24

~Jayna~

Just sitting in this office makes me sick. I can still see the look on Preston's face when he came in, uninvited, spewing all his crazy talk about me being his and finally getting what he's been wanting since I arrived.

Rebekah sits next to me, a hand on my back, rubbing gentle circles. "He is going to pay for this, Jayna. The HR manager was mortified when I called him and told him what had happened. I wouldn't be surprised if Preston is fired immediately."

I snort. "If only I could be so lucky. It sounds like he's gotten away with this kind of behavior before, which angers me to no end."

Rebekah nods. "Me, too."

The door opens and Mitch walks in. I feel like I can breathe again. He engulfs me in his arms. "You ready to get out of here, baby?"

"Yes, please."

Mitch looks over at Rebekah. "Thank you for all your help."

She smiles. "Go home and rest, Jayna. Don't worry about things here. We will take care of everything. The on-call doctors will cover as long as you need."

"Thank you, Rebekah. Can you fill Carrington in and tell him I'll talk to him soon?"

"Sure thing. I think he's out to lunch with his new man. He's going to be pissed that he wasn't here for you." Rebekah walks out, softly closing the door behind her.

Mitch pulls me into his strong embrace, holding me like he will never let me go.

"Please kiss me, Mitch. Make the thoughts of that man go away."

He swallows. "Did he..."

I shake my head. "No, but I'd hate to think how far he would have gone if you didn't come in."

That was all Mitch needed to hear as he gently kisses me, almost like he's afraid I'll break. All I need is the feeling of Mitch's lips to make me feel cherished.

"Do you need to get anything before we go?" he asks.

I grab my purse out of my desk and look around. "This is it." He grasps my hand and we walk out the back door.

"Are you sure you don't need to get back to work?" I ask.

He opens my door to his BMW, then climbs in. "That's the last place I want to be right now. I'm too angry. I need to process how I'm going to handle everything Maxon said to me."

"What did he say?"

"That asshole wanted me to make this 'go away'. He must be crazy if he thinks I'd ever try and talk you out of testifying."

"I don't want this to affect your position with the firm. You just made junior partner. I feel awful that you could be in trouble because of me."

He looks at me with warmth in his eyes. "Jayna, I love you as much today as I did the day we both went away to college. I choose you. Today, tomorrow, and for the rest of my life. I will forever live with the guilt of pushing you away. I was selfish. I knew you needed to devote your time to school, as did I. So I convinced myself that being apart was the best for both of us. I will never push you away again. You come before everything else."

I fling my arms around his neck. It's a good thing he hasn't started driving yet. "Oh, Mitch, I love you, too. So much. I don't want to dwell on the past. Maybe everything happened the way it was meant to. Otherwise I wouldn't have Michelle, and I couldn't imagine my life without her in it." I swallow, shaking my head. "Hopefully she won't notice anything is wrong when we Facetime later today."

"We can Facetime her together. That'll distract her."

"I'm so glad we found each other again."

He laughs. "Thank goodness for lazy Uber drivers."

"Yeah. If he would have helped me get my stuff out of the car, you never would have stopped to help."

"Fate brought us back together. Or maybe it was Starbucks." He shrugs. "We would've run into each other there eventually."

"I'd say it was your mother."

Mitch smiles. "You're probably right. She never pushed the issue when we were apart, but she told me she knew I'd see clearly again one day.

"So... Your place or mine?"

"I'd like to go to your place. I feel safer there."

"I'll always keep you safe."

Mitch weaves in and out of traffic like a pro. When he sees a Starbucks on the way, he smiles and pulls up to the drive-thru.

"You are the best." I lean over to kiss his cheek.

He hands me my cup. I take a sniff, moaning in appreciation.

"Hearing that almost makes me want to get one for myself." Mitch winks.

I raise my cup. "This right here is hard to beat."

He holds up a bag, waving it in front of my face. "Well, then, I guess I'll have to eat this lemon loaf by myself."

I snatch it from him. "Mocha with a side of lemon loaf is unbeatable."

Mitch's phone starts ringing through Bluetooth, the word *Work* flashing on the audio display. He pushes the ignore button.

"You can get that. What if it's something important?"

"Right now, you are the only thing that is important to me. Anything else can wait."

The song "Ocean" by Lady Antebellum comes on the radio. I turn it up. "Do you know how many times I've listened to this song since I first saw you again? I'm so glad you let me fall in deeper."

He smiles. "I'm glad you weren't afraid to drown."

I was so caught up in the song that I didn't realize when he pulled into the garage and parked. Mitch leans in and kisses the tears from my cheeks before exiting the car and rushing around to open my door.

Mitch doesn't let go of my hand the entire ride up the elevator or when he unlocks his door. He takes my purse and places it on the entryway table, then leads me to his luxurious bathroom.

"Let me run you a bath. It will help you relax."

"A bath sounds like heaven, but I don't have clothes."

"You can wear something of mine." Mitch hands me a towel. "Let me get the water going for you while you change out of your clothes."

I step into the bedroom and strip out of my clothes, wrapping the towel around me. When I re-enter the bathroom, the relaxing scent of lavender and vanilla permeates my nose. I look at Mitch, eyebrow raised.

He smiles. "The first time my dad and Marley came to visit, Marley left one of her bath bombs. I'm sure she won't mind that I let you enjoy it."

"You mean you don't have a secret bath bomb fetish?"

"Only if that fetish includes bath bombs and you." Mitch runs his index finger down my arm. "I'll be in the living room. Yell if you need me." He quietly closes the door.

I step into the tub and sink down into the water, immediately feeling the stress of the day melt away. I shut my eyes and lean back, my mind drifting to Mitch.

A knocking sound startles me.

"Come in."

Mitch slowly opens the door and walks in. "Jayna, are you okay? You've been in here for over an hour."

An hour?

I chuckle. "Now that you mention it, the water is quite cold, and I look like a prune. I must have drifted off. I'm sorry."

"You have nothing to be sorry for. If you're tired, you can take a nap. I placed a pair of boxer shorts and a t-shirt on the bed for you. I've put your clothes in the washing machine."

"Thanks, Mitch. I don't need a nap. It looks like I already took one."

He grabs my towel from the floor and hands it to me. I quickly stand and wrap it around my body, which is covered in goosebumps from not only the chill in the room, but Mitch's proximity. I carefully step out onto the bathmat.

"If you're hungry, I made sandwiches."

"Sandwiches sound perfect. I didn't realize how hungry I was."

"I even have your favorite Kettle brand chips. You got me addicted, so I keep them in my cabinet for when I crave something crunchy and salty."

I gasp. "Mr. Healthy keeps chips in his cabinet? I'm shocked."

"I'm not as healthy as you think. You're confusing me with my father. I'm a big fan of junk food." He rubs his eight-pack, as if it shows signs of fat.

I grab a hand towel off the sink to throw it at him, not thinking about the fact that I'm just wrapped in a towel myself. I hear Mitch moan as it unexpectedly falls to the floor. My nipples immediately harden at the look of need on his face.

"Jayna," he whispers.

"Mitch..."

"You're killing me here. I'm trying to be good, but *damn,* a man in love can only take so much."

"Say it again."

"*Damn.*"

I snort. "Not that part, smart ass."

He chuckles. "Oh, you mean the *man in love* part?" Mitch strides toward me, pulling my body against his. "I love you more than anything in this world. I won't lie and tell you I'm not thinking about all the dirty things I'd like to do to you, my tongue trailing over your body, but I want you to be the one in control."

"Yes, please," I pant.

"What?"

"Yes, please use your tongue on my body."

A guttural growl erupts from his chest as he drops to his knees and trails his tongue over my thighs. I know he can hear my breathing change, becoming heavier. "You smell so good, Jayna. I can smell your desire." He swipes his tongue through my wet folds, making me moan. "You taste even better than you smell."

I reach back and clutch the edge of the counter, feeling the orgasm building inside me. All it takes is one final flick of my clit and I come undone, wave after wave crashing around me. Mitch cups my ass to keep me from sinking to the floor as he begins to stand, placing kisses up my stomach and to my breasts. He swirls his tongue around my nipples, shooting desire to my core. Next, he nibbles his way up my neck to my jaw, making his way to my mouth. I can taste myself on his tongue, which turns me on even more.

I feel Mitch's need when he pulls my body to his. "Do you see how much I want you?"

"Yes. Take me. Please."

With those words, he scoops me up and carries me to his bed.

CHAPTER 25

~Mitch~

She looks like a goddess on my bed, dark, wet curls fanned out on my pillow. She's a vision that I've dreamt about for far too long. I could stare at her for hours.

"Mitch, you have entirely too much clothing on," Jayna says, pouting.

I rip my shirt open, not caring that several of the buttons just flew off. "Is this better?"

"Almost."

"Oh, you want me to take these off, too?" I tease, placing my hand on the waistband of my pants. "Let me get a condom first."

She shakes her head. "I'm on the pill and have been tested. I'm clean. I want to feel you without any barriers."

"Thank, fuck. I'm clean, too. I've never been without a condom and was just tested last month."

She gives me a seductive smile, nodding toward my pants. "Take them off, now!"

I unbuckle my slacks and let them fall to the floor. My need for her overcoming anything else, I pull my boxer briefs down and crawl up her naked body.

When she wraps her delicate hand around my hard cock, it's all I can do to not come right there. Being loved by the woman who consumes you mind, body, and soul is better than anything else in this world.

I position myself at her entrance and slowly enter her, placing my forehead against hers. "You're my everything. I love you, Jayna."

"I love you, too. This...us...our connection... It's the one piece of me that has been missing."

As we move in sync, expressing our love without words, our bodies respond as if no time has passed at all.

We both have tears rolling down our face as we come together as one.

We make love all afternoon. Finally, she falls asleep in my arms.

* * *

"How about a shower before we call Michelle."

"That sounds amazing." She raises her eyebrows suggestively.

That one look shoots a current straight to my dick. It's ready for round... Hell, I don't know. Five or six. After the first round of love-making, we were like horny teenagers.

She looks down at my growing erection as she stands. "Looks like *he* likes that idea, too."

My shower is massive, with jets and a rainfall showerhead.

I open the glass door and turn on the water, checking the temperature before gesturing for her to step in. I'll never tire of seeing her wet and naked in front of me.

"Look at all these jets!" she exclaims.

"Nothing relaxes you better than being sprayed hard with hot water," I say, a glint in my eye as I close the door behind us.

She takes a step back. "What are you thinking, Mitch Davis?"

She squeals when I grab her ass and lift her up so the spray hits her right on her clit.

"Oh god...," she moans.

When she starts panting, I know she's close. I step back and pull her away from the wall, turn her around and lean her forward so her hands are propped on the shower bench.

"Hold on, baby. It's going to be a fast, hard ride."

I slam into her from behind, wrapping my hands in her thick, wet hair as I thrust my hips.

"Come for me, Jayna," I say, giving one final tug on her hair as we both let go.

"Are you trying to kill me?" she pants.

"In all the best ways," I chuckle. "Sit down and let me wash you."

"It's a good thing you have this bench, because I don't think I could stand right now. Looks like I need to start hitting the gym if I'm going to be able to keep up with you."

"I'd love to see you all hot and sweaty at the gym with me, baby."

Jayna wears her own clothes now, which smell of me. I just might have given them a little squirt of my cologne after taking them out of the dryer. She talks to her mom while she waits for Michelle to come inside from flying kites with her dad.

I sit down beside her, wrapping my arm around her shoulders and smiling. She smiles back and blows me a kiss.

"Thanks, Mom."

Jayna pulls the phone from her ear and presses a button, then holds it in front of our faces. A ball energy explodes onto the screen.

"Hi, Mommy. I've missed you so much. Oh, Mr. Mitch. You're there, too. Mommy, are you at Mr. Mitch's house?"

"Yes. I'm spending the day with him."

"I wish I was there with you. I love Mr. Mitch."

I grasp Jayna's free hand and squeeze, my heart getting too large for my chest. "I love you, too, sweetheart. I promise, when you come home, you will be spending lots of time here with me and your mommy."

She starts jumping up and down, her face a blur on the screen. "Yeah! Did you hear that, Mimi and Pop? I get to spend time at Mr. Mitch's house, too."

Both of Jayna's parents come into the frame and smile. "It's good to see you, Mitch," her dad says. "I'm so glad you and Jayna have found your way back to each other. Her mother and I feel just awful about how we let things happen."

"That's water under the bridge. All that matters is we're back together now."

Michelle takes the phone back. "When are we going to Arkansas to see Mr. Benson and meet Emily and Marley?"

"Your mom and I will fly to get you in just a few more days, then we will fly to Arkansas and you can meet my entire family. They're going to love you so much." The smile on both Jayna's and Michelle's faces could light up the world.

It takes a few minutes and few hundred *I love yous* before either Jayna or Michelle are ready to hang up.

Once they do, I look at Jayna. "So, what do you want to do tonight?"

"Is it okay if we just snuggle on the couch? I have a few text messages from Carrington, Rebekah, and the HR manager I need to answer, then I'm all yours."

"Sounds good to me. I'll let you take care of that while I check in with Margaret and see if I need to take care of anything."

A look of worry crosses her face. I know she's afraid I'll lose my job. What she doesn't know is that I don't care. There will be other jobs, but only one Jayna.

I walk into my office, leaving the door open. I fall into my big leather chair and steel myself for the call, Margaret answering after two rings.

"Hi, Mitch. How are you holding up?"

I sigh. "I guess you've heard about what went down this afternoon."

"Let's just say there was a lot of yelling coming from Mr. Burns' office, your name being thrown out there a few times. It's a good thing the other partners were in court. I've never seen him like that. What happened?"

"Did you know he had a son?"

"Not until today."

"If the other partners stand by Maxon, I don't know how much longer I will be with the firm. I don't want to go into details, but I'm sure you will hear talk around the office. Will you please look on Mr. Jefferson's and Mr. Toone's calendars to see if they have any events listed that I might interrupt with a phone call?"

"Sure. Just give me a second." There's a brief pause. "Nothing is on the calendar for either one of them tonight."

"Thanks. You're the best. I'm not sure if I'll be in tomorrow or not. Did you schedule me to meet with any new clients?"

"No. You looked upset when you stormed out, so I haven't added anything to your calendar. You're off on Thursday and Friday, so I just waited to schedule new clients for next week."

"Wonderful. I may see you tomorrow if I come in to meet with the partners."

I send a text to both Mr. Jefferson and Mr. Toone to see if they're available for a conference call. Luckily, they both responded right away, agreeing to take my call.

This could be my future right here. Taking a deep breath, I call Mr. Toone first. "Good evening, Mr. Toone. Thank you for agreeing to take my call. Give me just a second to connect with Mr. Jefferson."

"Okay."

I connect to Mr. Jefferson, who doesn't even greet me before he starts right in.

"Davis, is everything okay? You usually just wait to talk to all of us until you get to the office. I assume Toone and Burns are on this call, as well."

"I'm sorry to bother both of you. It is just the three of us on this call."

Both men question at the same time, "Not Mr. Burns?"

"This is not a conversation I ever dreamed I'd be having with the senior partners. Where the *hell* do I begin?"

"Let us help you out with that," Mr. Jefferson starts. "We've already talked to Burns and stand by him. If you want to keep your position here, you need to convince your girlfriend to not testify against Preston. Maxon has worked hard to keep his name out of the press. He needs your loyalty as a junior partner."

Anger bubbles up inside me. "If you already know what's going on, why ask me if everything is okay? Are you testing me? If you are, this is a test I'm happy to fail. I'm sorry. I can't and won't ask Jayna to not testify. Take this as my resignation. I'll have a formal letter to you in the morning." It's all I can do to not tell them to fuck off. I'd throw my phone, but I don't want to break it or scare Jayna.

CHAPTER 26

~Jayna~

I pull the phone away from my ear to keep my eardrums from bursting when Carrington yells, "Why the *hell* didn't you tell me Dr. Joseph was harassing you? I would've kicked his ass. Are you okay? Did your sexy beau come in and save the day like Rebekah said he did?"

"Slow down. You're making my head hurt. First off, I tried to take care of it without involving anybody else." I smile. "And yes, my sexy man came in and saved the day."

"There was a memo from HR stating that Preston was on administrative leave until further notice and that we'll have a new doctor filling in for him."

"I think his stunt today left them with no choice. Rebekah told me there's been a lot of turnover at the clinic, especially among female staff. Do you think he had something to do with that?"

"It wouldn't surprise me a bit. I am a bit shocked no one else has filed a complaint."

"I have a feeling his daddy has paid people to keep their mouth shut. I hate that Mitch is working for a man as vile as what Maxon Burns appeared to be."

I hear somebody clear their throat and look up, seeing Mitch leaning against the wall. Great. "Hey, Carrington, I need to go. I'll call you later."

I hang up and open my mouth to explain, but Mitch holds up his hand with a smile.

"You and me both, baby. That is why I resigned, effective immediately."

My eyes widen. "*What?* You can't do that. You've worked too hard to get where you are."

"I can't work for people who expect me to brush something like this under the rug. Both Toone and Jefferson told me to do what Burns said and convince you to not testify. I would never dream of that. I love you and you're my priority. Not the firm. There will be other jobs. Hell, maybe I'll even open my own practice. Divorce law doesn't have the same appeal to me as it did before."

The tears cascade down my face. "You are my hero."

"I want to be that and more, if you'll let me."

I run and jump into his arms. He has never owned my heart more than he does right now.

Mitch wipes my eyes with his thumbs and pushes the hair out of my face. "Don't cry, baby. This is for the best. I don't want you to ever second-guess that you come first. I know you had no reason to trust that before. I was young and stupid when I put my fears first. That will never happen again."

"I do trust you, Mitch. I love you so much."

"I love you." His words are strong and unwavering. "So, how did your calls go?"

"Rebekah just kept saying she was sorry and that she should have realized something was going on with him. I don't blame her. Charles swears I'm the first person to file a complaint with HR. All I can guess is that Preston or his father paid off the other employees to not say anything.

"To be honest, I just want to forget this ever happened. As much as I like my job, I'll probably start looking for something somewhere else. Charles gave me the rest of the week off, which is only two days, since I already took Thursday and Friday off to get Michelle in Ohio and then go to Arkansas to see your family."

"*Our* family, Jayna. They are just as much your family as they are mine."

"They feel like it. I can't wait to meet Emily and Kristi. I have stories I want to tell her about Henry."

Mitch laughs. "Oh, please do. That would make my day. I'm going to call Dad and let him know what happened. He'll be mad as hell if I wait until we get there to tell him."

"I hope he won't be mad that you no longer have a job."

"Jayna, once he finds out what they want me to do, he'd be furious if I *stayed*. Put that out of your head. I must admit, I almost feel a sense of relief at knowing I'm no longer working there. Like I said, being a divorce lawyer was never really what I wanted to do. I wanted to be a business lawyer, like Henry."

"You can do whatever you put your mind to, Mitch Davis. You're the most brilliant man I know." Smart doesn't even begin to describe him.

"You've always been my biggest fan and supporter. Well, up until I was an idiot..." He smiles, "which we will no longer talk about."

"Sounds good to me. That's in the past. The future is all I'm looking forward to."

CHAPTER 27

~Mitch~

I slide out of bed to grab a quick shower. I'm ready to get this over with. I typed my resignation letter last night and plan on leaving it on Maxon's desk this morning. The worst part about leaving is not seeing Margaret every day. She's been like a mother to me since I started working for the firm.

When I finish getting dressed and walk into the kitchen, I'm surprised to see Jayna holding out a cup of coffee to me. "Why are you up already?"

She shrugs. "When your warmth left me, I woke up. You've spoiled me. It's going to be hard to sleep without you next to me."

I tilt my head. "We need to do something about that." I want her and Michelle with me all the time. I need to work on making that happen.

"You might sing a different tune when an almost three-year-old jumps on the bed at six thirty every morning." She laughs.

"Naw, that will just get me up and to the gym earlier. More time to spend with you."

She smiles. "Where are you headed so early this morning?"

"I'm going to the office to turn in my resignation letter and clean out my desk. I want to get this over with."

"Does it make you sad?"

I shrug. "Not really. The only thing that makes me sad is leaving Margaret. She's been like a mother to me."

"I'm sorry, Mitch. I know she's going to miss you."

I drain the cup and place it into the sink. "Thank you for the coffee, sweetheart. I'll be back soon. Make yourself at home."

"I'll be waiting for you."

Traffic looks a lot different this time of day than it does at eight thirty. Very few people are out and about at six thirty.

I pull into a parking space right in front of the building in the one-hour parking. I won't be here long, so I don't have to worry about getting a ticket.

The smell of coffee greets me when I walk into the building. I wave at the baristas in the Starbucks as I pass by. I'm sure they are wondering why I'm here so early and why I didn't stop in.

When I get off the elevator on the fortieth floor, I'm shocked to see Margaret sitting at her desk, a sad expression on her face. "Margaret, what are you doing here so early?"

"After I talked to you yesterday, I had a bad feeling. You are an honorable man. This firm was never really the right fit for you. I love you like a son and told myself I'd look out for you. Mr. Burns is not a good man. He has done many things over the years that I've questioned, but I can't afford to lose my job, so I've kept my mouth shut."

"You have been so good to me, Margaret. I guess I had blinders on, only seeing my desire to make partner. It wasn't until fate stepped in that I saw what I've been blind to. I just can't work with a man like Maxon Burns. Can you believe he wants me to convince my girlfriend to not testify against his son for assaulting her?"

Her eyes widen. "His son *assaulted* your girlfriend?"

I nod. "He's a physician in the clinic here in this building. Jayna also works there. He has been hitting on her and making inappropriate comments, which quickly escalated to threats. He cornered her in her office yesterday and assaulted her."

"Oh, my goodness, Mitch. I'm so sorry."

"When I tried to talk to the other partners, they told me to make it *go away*, so I told them I was resigning. That's why I'm here. To pack up my stuff and leave this letter..." I hold up the envelope, "on Maxon's desk. I want to be out of here before they arrive."

Margaret stands and makes her way around the desk, embracing me in a motherly hug. "I'm going to miss you so much. It's not going to be the same without you here. Please, keep in touch."

"I will. I promise." I squeeze her, then go into Mr. Burns' office and drop the letter on top of his desk. I quickly make my way to my office to pack up the few personal items I have. It's really only some law books and my degree, which I place into a box.

I'm in and out in less than twenty minutes. I stop in Starbucks to pick up a skinny mocha for Jayna and a double-shot espresso for me. The barista looks at the box in my hand. "I saw you coming in early, and now you're leaving with a box. Are you moving?"

"No. Just decided it was time for a change."

"Here," she says with a smile, handing me both cups. "On the house."

I thank her and drop a twenty into the tip jar.

I climb into my car, then call Jayna to see if she needs me to pick up anything on my way home.

She answers on the first ring. "Hello, handsome. Did everything go okay?"

"Everything went fine. Margaret had a feeling something was going to happen today, so she came in early and was waiting. It was hard saying goodbye to her. As for everyone else, I was in and out quickly and didn't see anybody. I just wanted to see if you needed me to pick up anything...besides a skinny mocha. I already have that for you."

She squeals. "You're the sweetest. No, I'm good. I ate a bagel. I hope that's okay. It was your last one."

"Of course. You're welcome to anything you want at my place." I'd give her the moon if I could. How could I possibly be upset about her eating my last bagel? "I'm just a few blocks from home. I love you."

"Love you, too."

CHAPTER 28

~Jayna~

Today we fly to Ohio to pick up Michelle. I must admit, I'm a little nervous about my parents and Mitch being in the same space. After all, it was their decision to keep his mother's cancer diagnosis from me. I know they were only thinking of my future and didn't think how it would affect him.

I spent the whole week at Mitch's house. Tuesday, he took me back to my place to pack a bag for the week and for the trip. Mom told me not to worry about packing Michelle anything, because they went on a little shopping trip.

"Mitch, can you help me bring my bag into the living room?"

"I'll be right there. I was just getting our Uber set."

"I need your muscle power."

"Why doesn't that surprise me?" he says as he walks into the bedroom. "The Uber will be here in less than five minutes. You ready to head down?"

"Yes. I have everything in that bag and my carry-on."

Mitch slings my carry-on over his shoulder, then pulls out the handle on my bag and stacks his on top, pulling them down the hall and out the door. "Can you shut the door for me, babe? My hands are just a little full." He smirks.

"I could've grabbed my carry-on bag," I shoot right back.

Our ride pulls up just as we walk outside. My eyes widen as I look at Mitch. "An Audi A6? Really? A normal car isn't good enough?"

"What can I say? You know how long it takes to get to the airport. We might as well have a smooth, quiet ride."

"I can't argue with you there."

Mitch helps our driver load our luggage into the trunk, then opens the door for me. He climbs in the other side and reaches for my hand, entwining our fingers. "Did you know my mom had an Audi? It was her dream car."

"I sure did. Even though we weren't together when she got it, she called and told me all about it. We talked at least once a month, then she just stopped calling. That was about the time she found out she was sick. It wouldn't surprise me if she stopped calling to keep me from finding out, knowing I would leave school to come back home."

"I had no idea you two kept in touch. She loved you so much, Jayna. I know she is rejoicing at the fact I pulled the stick out of my ass." He laughs.

The ride to the airport seems to take forever, but we left in plenty of time to make our flight.

"Do you care if we stop somewhere for a drink?" I ask as Mitch grabs our bags out of the trunk. "I get a little nervous when I fly. Michelle loves to fly and thinks it's funny that I close my eyes at take-off and landing."

Mitch smiles as he checks our bags, then leads me through security and to the first pub we see. We take a seat at the end of the bar.

"What would you like to drink?" he asks.

"White wine, please. Just a little something to help me relax."

"Are you sure that's strong enough?" he asks as he signals the bartender.

The female bartender eyes Mitch appreciatively, not even looking my way. "What can I get for you, hot stuff?"

Mitch looks over at me, seeing my nostrils flare. He quickly responds, "My girlfriend would like a Pinot Grigio, and I'll take an Angry Orchard."

Only then does she look at me. "Sure. I'll be right back."

I glare at her back as she walks away. "I can't believe that woman acted like I wasn't even sitting here. How many men do you think she hits on every day that are either married or in a relationship? That just sickens me."

"You are all I see, so it doesn't matter." He chuckles. "Do you know what this reminds me of?"

I cross my arms over my chest. "What?"

"Think about it. Remember that clerk at the inn I took you to after you turned eighteen? You were about ready to kick her ass."

I bust out laughing. "Oh, my gosh. I forgot all about that. She was, like, ten years older than you. Stupid tramp."

The bartender returns with our drinks, placing mine in front of me and turning to Mitch. "Here ya go, sugar."

It takes everything in me to keep my mouth shut. Mitch leans in, placing a tender kiss on my lips and whispering, "Don't do it."

We go over our plans for the day while we sip on our drinks, finishing just in time to hear the first-class boarding call for our flight. "Here goes nothing," I mumble as I drink my last sip of wine.

Mitch stands, offering me his hand to help me up. "We can get you another glass after we board."

"I'm good. I just needed that one to relax."

We walk hand and hand down the terminal to our gate. The attendant takes our boarding pass as we enter. Mitch leads me to our seats, sensing my anxiety as he buckles his lap belt. He grabs my hand as we taxi down the runway and take off, squeezing to ease my fears.

Having his calming presence next to me must have relaxed me

because, before I know it, Mitch gently shakes my shoulder to wake me up. "We are about to land, sweetheart."

I clear my throat. "Thank you." I sit up and reach for his hand in preparation for landing. I look out the window, seeing the runway coming closer.

The best part about sitting in first class is being able to disembark first. I practically drag Mitch off the plane.

Michelle is the first to see us coming down the walkway. "Mommy!" She runs and jumps into my arms, giving me a big hug. "Hi, Mr. Mitch. Are you glad to see me, too?"

"Hi, sweet girl. I am *so* glad to see you. I've missed you."

"Did you hear that Mimi? Pop? Mr. Mitch missed me, too."

Mom pulls me in for a hug, while Dad reaches out to shake Mitch's hand.

"I hope you haven't been waiting too long," I say.

"We just got here. Your flight was right on time," Dad replies.

Mom whispers into my ear, "You are glowing, baby. You look so happy."

"I am, Mom. Happier than I've been in a very long time."

Dad places his hand on Mitch's shoulder. "Thank you for getting my girl here safely. It's good to see you, son."

"It was my pleasure, Mr. Shipman."

Dad laughs. "Just because it's been years since we've seen each other, I'm still Matt. If you call Gloria Mrs. Shipman, you will make her feel old, so I'm going to warn you now."

Mom swats Dad on the arm. "Get over here, Mitch, and give me a hug."

Michelle claps. "Everybody loves Mr. Mitch."

CHAPTER 29

~Mitch~

Seeing that precious little girl running toward us just did something to me. Having them both with me makes me feel whole. One day soon, I hope to make both her and Jayna mine forever. Being here is the perfect opportunity to let Matt and Gloria know how I feel. I'm going to ask their blessing to make them my family. I don't need it, but I want it.

Michelle reaches from Jayna to me. "Hold me, Mr. Mitch. I'm getting so big I might hurt Mommy, but you got big muscles. I know I won't hurt you."

I take her in my arms. "You are a big girl, but I don't think you'll ever be too big for your Mommy to hold you."

"Mimi drove the minivan. Maybe she'll let you drive," Michelle says sweetly, wiggling out of my arms and running over to her. I'm sure she is going to ask her to let me drive.

Jayna laughs.

"What's so funny?" I ask, eyes narrowed.

"Please drive it. I can't tell you the number of fantasies I've had featuring you driving a minivan."

"Are you serious?"

She nods. "It all started when you took Michelle and me out for pizza that first time. Don't you remember Michelle saying you should get a minivan?"

"I forgot all about that. So..." I waggle my brows. "I've been in your dreams?"

"You're the *star* of all my dreams, hot stuff."

I lean closer and lower my voice. "Stop. I'm getting hard. Which isn't something I want to explain to Michelle or your parents."

"I'm sorry. I'll be good."

I swat her ass. "You'd better be."

Michelle comes running back. "Mimi said you can drive if you want, Mr. Mitch."

"That's okay, sweetheart. I'll let your pop drive. He will get us there faster."

"Pop doesn't drive fast. Mimi does."

She giggles when Gloria picks her up and tickles her. "You're not supposed to tell everything you know, you little toot."

We all walk out and climb into the van. Jayna sits next to Michelle, and her mom climbs into the back. "Mitch, you sit up front with Matt. You'll have more legroom up there."

"Gloria, I feel horrible sitting up here and you in the back. I don't mind. It's only a thirty-minute drive."

"Nonsense. I'm fine back here. No arguments."

"Yes, ma'am."

Matt looks at me, eyebrow raised. "Good decision. I haven't won an argument in almost thirty years."

"My dad always let my mom think she won. But I think he won more than she thought."

He smiles. "Your dad's a smart man." Matt clears his throat. "I want to thank you for helping Jayna with what happened. I wish she would've told us what was going on. I would've flown into town and let him have a piece of my mind. I feel horrible that you gave up your partnership, though."

"You don't ever have to thank me for taking care of Jayna. I would give up anything to protect her. And I think leaving the firm was the best thing that could have happened."

I glance over my shoulder to see Jayna has moved to sit next to her mom, the two women deep in conversation, while Michelle has on her headphones and is watching the DVD.

"Matt, I love Jayna and Michelle. I'd like nothing more than to have your blessing to ask her to be my wife."

Matt nods with a smile. "Son, I've always known you were who God chose for our daughter. I hate that we were the cause of you two being apart for so many years, but then again, I think God has a plan for all things. That is why you are sitting next to me now. I know you'll take good care of my girls and would love to have you as a son-in-law." He reaches over and pats my knee.

"Thank you, Matt. That means a lot. I don't blame you for what happened between Jayna and I. My stubborn streak and fear of being hurt like my dad was what kept me from reaching out to her and apologizing for how I acted. That's on me. I will live the rest of my life putting her first. I can promise you that."

When Jayna's phone rings, she sucks in a breath, holding it up. "It's the prosecutor's office." The car goes quiet while she answers.

A few moments later, she hangs up. "That was Mr. Ballard, the head prosecutor. He told me they are charging Preston with stalking. Do you agree with that, Mitch?"

"Stalking is a third-degree felony. A first offense carries a prison sentence of two to ten years and a maximum fine of $10,000. You can also file a restraining order to keep him from having future contact with you. I'm thrilled that they went with stalking over harassment. Harassment is just a misdemeanor with minimal jail time, if any."

"Mr. Ballard wasn't sure when it would go to trial, but wanted to know if I'd be willing to testify. I told him absolutely. I'm ready for this to be over."

"I know, sweetheart. We are one step closer."

Jayna blows out a breath. "It could be months before this goes to trial, so let's just put it out of our minds and enjoy our time together."

"I couldn't agree more."

Michelle looks up when we pull into her grandparents' driveway and squeals. "Look, Mr. Mitch. We're here. This is where Mimi and Pop live."

I smile back at her. "I know, sweetheart. I've known your mommy for a long time. I've been at this house lots of times."

Michelle has a look of surprise on her face, her mouth open and nose scrunched up. "You have?"

"Yep, but you can show me around. I'm sure some things have changed since I was last here."

Our flight to Arkansas leaves early tomorrow morning, so after we unload our stuff, get the grand tour from Michelle, and visit for a while, Jayna and I decide to head to the cemetery to visit Mom.

We sit on the couch, Michelle on my lap. "Sweetheart, your mom and I are going to go somewhere for a little bit. We will be back soon, and I'll maybe even bring you a surprise."

She scrunches up her face. "You're leaving? But you just got here."

"We're not leaving. We're just going to visit my mother at the cemetery." I feel like a fish out of water. I don't know how to explain death to a child.

Jayna grasps my hand, jumping in. "Baby, do you remember us talking about heaven when you asked about my grandparents?"

"Yes, Mommy. You said it's the most beautiful place where everyone is happy and nobody is sick or in pain. If you're a good person, that's where you go when you die. Like Gramps and Memaw."

"That's right, baby. Well, Mitch's mommy got really sick a long time ago and went to heaven."

"Then how you going to visit her? You said we can't go to heaven until we die."

"We aren't actually going to visit her, but a place. You will understand one day."

"Okay, Mommy." She then looks at me, placing a hand on my arm. "I'm sorry your mommy is in heaven, Mr. Mitch. I love you."

"Thank you, sweet pea. I love you, too."

Jayna's dad walks in and throws me the keys to his truck. "I'm sure you'd rather drive this instead of that minivan."

"Thanks, Matt. We won't be gone too long."

"Take your time, son."

On our way to the cemetery, we stop by the florist to get my mom's favorite flowers, pink gerbera daisies, then Starbucks. She'd be upset if we didn't have one in her memory.

The cemetery is beautiful. I know my dad pays extra to keep her plot clean and covered in fresh flowers. My chest heavy, tears start to build in my eyes the closer we drive to her plot. As soon as I put the truck in park, Jayna pulls me into her arms, giving me strength. We sit there for a minute, holding each other, lost in our thoughts. Then we both slide out of my side of the truck and walk hand in hand to her final resting place. A warm breeze blows through the trees. We kneel in front of her beautiful granite headstone.

Placing the flowers on top, I swallow. "Hi, Mom. I'm sorry I haven't been here to see you. I've been a stubborn fool, but I promise you, I'm no longer that man. Look who is here with me?"

Jayna wipes a tear from her eye. "Hi, Em. The last time I was here, I spilled my heart out to you. I was lost, scared, but talking to you made things not so terrifying. I'm in a totally different place now, and I'm pretty sure I have you to thank for it."

I smile. "Mom, did you bring Jayna back to me? It's the only explanation of how we found each other again. You and fate had a little talk and decided it was time for me to wake up, didn't you? I promise to be the man you can be proud of. The man you raised me to be. Jayna is the most amazing mother. You should see her little girl.

Michelle. We are taking her to meet the family tomorrow. She already met dad when he came to see me last month." I chuckle. "You should have seen her face as she looked back and forth between the two of us. The older I get, the more I look like him."

I run my hand along the smooth granite and stand, holding my hand out for Jayna. "I promise to not wait so long next time. You are always in my heart." I tap my hand over my heart. "I love you so much."

"I love you, Emily," Jayna whispers.

I take Jayna's hand and bring it up to my lips, giving her a tender kiss. "Are you ready to go, sweetheart?"

"Whenever you are."

As we walk away, I turn back for one more look at my mom's headstone, feeling better than I have in a long time.

* * *

Michelle is a bundle of excitement as we disembark the plane. "How long will it take to get to Mr. Benson's house? Do you think Emily will play with me? Does she have dolls?"

I smile. "They don't live very far. Emily will be so excited to play with you and share her toys. She's talked about it every time I've spoken to her on the phone."

Jayna squeezes Michelle's hand. "Mommy is excited, too." Then she looks at me. "I haven't seen Henry in a long time. I feel like I know Marley, but I've never met her in person."

"That's right. Mom invited Marley to our high school graduation, but she ended up getting sick."

"It's crazy that we were together for five years and I never met her in person. Now she is married to your dad. Life throws us so many unexpected twists and turns."

We grab our luggage from baggage claim, then make our way to the rental car area. I smirk, thinking about the look on Jayna's face when she sees what kind of car I've rented. I step up to the counter and give the representative my information.

She smiles, handing me the key fob. "Here you go, Mr. Davis. You will find your car in row f, space three."

"Thank you. Jayna, you and Michelle sit on the bench right over there while I get the car."

"Okay. Thank you."

"Thanks, Mr. Mitch," Michelle yells.

When I pull up, Jayna laughs and Michelle jumps up and down when she sees the black Nissan Quest minivan.

"You got us a minivan, Mr. Mitch. I knew you would like one like Mimi has."

I open the sliding door, and she jumps right in. "I even rented a fancy car seat for you." I touch the tip of her nose. "And look." I point to the screen above her seat. "There's already a movie playing."

Her grin is infectious. I look at Jayna, who is also smiling. Her smile turns flirty as she looks me up and down, licking her bottom lip. She walks closer and gets on her tiptoes. "You have me thinking very naughty things," she whispers as she nips my ear and climbs into the front seat.

Fuck, how does she do that? I'm going to get a hard-on every time I leave an airport now. It's a good thing I'm wearing jeans and not athletic pants, although athletic pants would be a lot less restrictive on my dick right now. Jayna still has a grin on her face when I get in and try to adjust myself.

"Vixen," I whisper.

Michelle's excitement saves me from continual torture from Jayna on the drive to my dad's house. She asks a million questions about my family, especially Emily. She can't wait to meet her and play with all her *big girl* toys.

When I slow down to turn into my dad's driveway, Jayna sucks in a breath. "Wow. This is a beautiful house."

"Dad wanted to have something new to both him and Marley, so they built this house, then Henry and Kristi bought Marley's house. It worked out well for everybody."

"Is Henry's house close?"

"Less than a mile away."

"That's wonderful. Kristi is probably happy to have family so close by. Don't her parents live in Conway? How far is that?"

"Depends on who's driving." I laugh. "It's a little over two hours, I think."

"That's not too bad. I'm sure her parents burn up the roads coming to visit."

Michelle looks up from her movie and squeals. "We're here! Look at that big swing set and playhouse, Mommy."

Jayna nods. "That looks like fun. You and Emily will have a lot of fun playing on there."

As soon as I shut my car door, Emily comes running down the front steps, with Dad and Marley following close behind, and crashes into my legs. "Mitch, I've missed you. I'm so happy you came to see me."

"Hi, squirt. I've missed you, too. Now, let go of my leg so I can get Michelle out of the van. She's been dying to meet you."

I look over to the passenger side and see my dad's arms around Jayna, both smiling. With a giggle, Marley pushes my dad out of the way and pulls Jayna into a hug. I hit the button to open the rear driver's side door and make quick work of unbuckling Michelle.

As soon as her feet hit the ground, she runs up to Emily, looking up and smiling. "Hi! You a big girl. Mommy says I'm getting big, but you way taller than me. I love your dress."

"Hi, Michelle. I'm almost five. I'll be in kindergarten soon." She spins. "I'm wearing my dance leotard tutu. I've been practicing for my recital tomorrow. I'm so happy you came to see me dance."

Michelle looks at Jayna. "Mommy, can I have a toot toot?"

Jayna does her best to hold in her laugh. "*Tutu.* And yes, if you want to try dancing, like Emily, you'll get one."

Emily smiles. "She can have some of my old ones that don't fit me anymore. That's okay, isn't it, Mom?"

Marley nods. "Of course. I bet we have a bunch we can let Michelle have."

Michelle's eyes grow wide. "Did you hear that, Mommy? She said I can have lots."

"What do you say, baby?"

This interaction makes me even more certain that the sooner I can make Jayna mine forever, the better.

"Thank you, thank you, thank you." Michelle rushes to hug both Emily and Marley. Dad's face matches mine. Love, pride, and happiness all rolled into one.

Dad clears his throat. "You girls go inside. Mitch and I will bring in the bags. Henry and Kristi will be here shortly. Kristi had her sixteen-week appointment today. The doctor told them she may be able to tell the sex of the baby. Last I heard, they were still fighting over finding out. Henry wants to wait, and Kristi wants to know."

"Well, seeing as Henry can't say no to Kristi, sounds like we may know the gender of the baby shortly." I laugh.

Dad pats my back, smirking. "I think you're probably right, son. That's why I have sparkling white grape juice and champagne chilling in the fridge. Marley had the cutest EM Fitness onesies made. One pink and one blue. That way, we have both our bases covered."

I look to make sure the girls have gone inside. "By the way, you were right, Dad. I think I'm more in love with Jayna today than I was the day she left for Harvard. She is the most remarkable mother and doctor. She has strength, determination, and a heart full of forgiveness and love. I plan to ask her to marry me. I feel like it's long overdue. It's like no time has passed at all, yet a lifetime at the same time."

He smiles. "Looks like we will have several reasons to celebrate. You know I have your mother's engagement and wedding rings. She wanted you to have them. They're in my office. I will give them to you to do with as you see fit."

I blink back the tears. "Thank you, Dad. That's perfect. I know Jayna will cherish them."

When we walk inside, Dad takes the bags from my hands and carries them up to our room. Marley and Jayna take pictures and laugh at the girls, who now wear matching tutus. Emily is trying to teach Michelle basic feet positioning, but she is too busy twirling around. Hopefully Emily has more patience than her big brother used to. I have a feeling I wasn't so tolerant at that age. At least if you listen to stories from Henry.

The door flies open and Kristi comes rushing in. "It's a boy!" she says excitedly. Henry walks in, shaking his head.

"Dad said you didn't want to find out, bro. Then again, we all know who wears the pants in your family," I tease and pull him into a hug.

"Hardy har har. There was no mistaking what was between my boy's legs. The ultrasound tech didn't even have to tell me. I could see it."

"Henry..." Kristi laughs. "The tech said that was the umbilical cord. His penis wasn't even in view when you got all excited."

I bite my bottom lip to keep from laughing. "You'd better come give me a hug, little momma." I wrap my arms around her. "You look beautiful. Pregnancy definitely agrees with you."

"Thank you, Mitch. I'm loving every minute of it. Ask me again in a couple of months, though, and I may be singing a different tune."

"Jayna, get over here!" yells Henry. "I want to get an overdue hug and introduce you to my beautiful wife."

Jayna scrunches up her face. "Eww... I don't want to hug you."

"Mommy," Michelle says, exasperated. "That's not nice."

"I was just teasing Henry, sweetheart. He's like a little brother to me."

"If *I* had a little brother, I would be nice and give him lots and lots of hugs." She frowns. "When can I have a little brother?"

This catches Jayna off guard. "Woah. Where did that come from? We'll talk about that another time, sweetie."

I can't help but think, *Hopefully sooner rather than later.*

Dad comes into the living room, a knowing glint in his eye. He walks by me, slipping me a small box as he passes. It's like he can read my mind. He makes his way across the room and pulls Marley into his chest, wrapping his arms around her. My dad has always loved with everything he has. I'm planning to be just like him.

Kristi sticks her hand out. "Hi, Jayna. It's nice to meet you. Henry has told me all about you. Your little girl is just beautiful. She looks just like you."

"I'm a hugger," Jayna says, looking at her hand. "Do you mind if I give you a hug?"

They laugh and embrace like old friends. "I am, too," says Kristi, "but I didn't want to just assume. Welcome to the Davis Circus."

"I'm well aware of the shenanigans that go on in this house. These two," she says, jerking a thumb at me and Henry, "kept me on my toes. Even Benson had a prankster streak in him from time to time."

"I love her already." Kristi nods at me with approval.

Marley directs us all into the kitchen, where she has set out little yellow cupcakes surrounding the blue onesie. Dad brings out the bubbly and plastic champagne glasses. He pours himself, Kristi, and the kids the sparkling white grape juice, the rest of us the champagne.

He raises his glass. "To my first grandson. We can't wait to meet you. Henry and Kristi, thank you for bringing another Davis boy into the world. Being a parent is the best gift ever, but I hear being a grandparent is even better."

I'm happy for Henry, but a small part is jealous. Jayna looks over at me, then down at her feet. *Shit.* Does she feel bad that Michelle isn't mine?

CHAPTER 30

~Jayna~

I look over at Mitch, seeing the same sadness on his face that I'm sure is on mine. We thought we'd be the first to give Benson grandchildren. It hurts my heart that I couldn't give this to him.

Mitch walks over and grasps my hand, leads me out to the back deck, and shuts the door. "Stop it, Jayna. I know we both thought it would be us giving him the first grandchild, but if I have my way, we have."

I frown. "What are you talking about?"

"This isn't exactly how I had things planned, but…" He takes a deep breath. "I love you and Michelle. She is already a part of me, blood or not. I can't explain it, but I felt like she was mine the second I met her. I want you to be my wife. I want to be her daddy. I may not be her biological dad and my dad may not be her grandfather, but there will never be a day that passes when she will ever feel that way. We will love her as fiercely as if she was born into this family. Marry me, Jayna, and become my life, my wife, my everything."

Tears stream down my face at his beautiful words. I don't even have to think about it. This is what I've wanted since I was sixteen.

I throw my arms around him. "Yes, yes, a million times yes. You are the man of my dreams. Time, distance, and some bumps in the road haven't changed how I feel about you. I would be honored to be your wife. And I want nothing more than for Michelle to have you as her father. I love you, Mitch."

Mitch pulls back and gets down on one knee, a blue box in his hand. I gasp, covering my mouth when he pulls out Emily's engagement ring.

"Jayna, will you be my wife?"

"Yes."

He slides on the ring, his smile radiant. "It fits, like it was meant to be."

When Benson opens the back door, we hear cheers from everyone inside. He walks out. "One of the last things Emily said to me was, if Mitch ever found his way back to you, she wanted him to give you this ring."

Happy tears still fall from my eyes. Michelle runs up to me. "Mommy, you not supposed to be crying. Everyone is happy."

"Mommy *is* happy, baby." I kneel. "Do you want us to be a family? Do you want Mitch to be your daddy?"

She looks at me, eyes wide, tears forming. "Yes, Mommy. I've never had a daddy, and I love Mr. Mitch so much." She looks at him. "Are you really my daddy now?"

"Yes, sweetheart, if you'll take me," he says, wiping tears from her face.

Two months ago, as I packed to move to Dallas, if anybody would have asked me if I thought I'd be engaged and more in love than I'd thought possible, I would have told them they were crazy. I thought my chance at true love ended a long time ago. I couldn't have been more wrong. Fate certainly takes you on a wild ride.

Henry comes out and breaks me from my thoughts. "Well, looks like Benny is going to have a cousin. Welcome to the family, sis."

"Thank you, Henry. And Benny? Is that what you're naming the baby?"

"His full name is Benson Henry Davis, but we are going to call him Benny until he tells us we can't."

"That's a wonderful name, Henry. And I'm shocked, but happy. I had no idea Mitch was going to do this."

"I say it's about damn time." He pulls me toward the door. "Come on. Let's celebrate all the new members coming into the Davis family."

Michelle is so excited. Benson tells her she can call him Papaw and Marley Nana if she wants. I almost start crying again, the tears falling freely when Michelle yells, "Daddy, come watch me and Emily dance."

Marley wraps her arms around me. "Honey, your little girl will know love like no other. I have loved Mitch and Henry since the day they were born. Their mother was my best friend, so they have always felt like a part of me. One thing about love is that it knows no bounds, especially when you are raised with nothing but love."

"I don't feel like it's real just yet."

She smiles. "Get ready, because you know as well as I do that Mitch will want to make this official sooner rather than later. You'd better give your parents a call. I'm sure they will want to know all about it."

Crap. I was so happy, I never even thought about that.

I walk back outside and pull out my cell phone. Mom answers on the first ring.

"Hi, baby. I was starting to get worried. You were supposed to land a couple hours ago."

"I'm sorry, Mom. It's been a very exciting day. Is Dad there with you?"

"He's sitting right here."

"Can you put the phone on speaker? I need to tell you both something." I look up, seeing Mitch walking out, a grin on his face. "Dad, Mom, well... Mitch asked me to marry him and I said yes," I rush out, then blow out a breath.

Mitch takes the phone. "I know I told you I was planning on asking her, but I'm sure you weren't expecting it to be today. I wasn't, either, but it just felt right. Like I told you, Matt. I love your girls with everything in me. I plan on being the best husband and father anybody could want for their daughter. Get ready, because I don't plan on this being a long engagement. Michelle asked us today when she can have a baby sister or brother." He hands me back the phone and winks.

"So... Say something."

"We are so happy for you, baby girl. Your mom is speechless. She's crying happy tears. Mitch had asked me for permission to marry you when y'all were here. I'm not really surprised. He looks more in love with you now than he did when you were younger."

Mom, sniffing, grabs the phone and tells Dad to go back to watching tv because she has a wedding to plan.

"Mom, calm down, I don't need a big wedding. I just want to be his wife.

"Listen, I need to go back inside. Henry just found out they are having a little boy, and we were celebrating the news when Mitch popped the question. I'll call you soon. I love you both so much."

"Love you, too, baby," comes from both Mom and Dad. "Bye."

* * *

We are the loudest family at the dance recital. Benson made sure we got there early so we'd have seats in the front row. Michelle was thrilled, saying she was *close enough to touch* the dancers. She looks so cute wearing a tutu and some ballet slippers Marley found. Looks like we will be signing her up for dance lessons.

I'm going to be so sad when we have to leave to go back home. Michelle loves it and acts like she's lived here all her life. She's already attached to Benson, taking his suggestion to call him Papaw. He is eating it up, too. She hasn't called Mitch by his name once since he told her he wanted to be her daddy. He is Daddy to her now.

Emily's performance was flawless. This child was made to dance. She was the youngest dancer to have a solo. You can see the pride on Benson's, Mitch's, and Henry's faces. I feel sorry for her and Michelle when they get older, because every boy who likes them will have to get past three very intimidating men.

After the recital, Mitch says, "Where do you want to go eat?"

"I know what I want," Henry responds.

"Lead the way, bro. I bet we are on the same page."

We end up at what Mitch and Henry call the best sandwich shop around. Hammontree's Grilled Cheese. I never dreamed you could make grilled cheese so many different ways, let alone dedicate a business to it.

I laugh when I see Marley climbing out of the driver's seat of her new Tesla. Looks like Benson isn't getting to drive it like he thought he would.

I look at the building and shake my head. *Watch out Hammontree's. Here we come.*

CHAPTER 31

~Mitch~

While the girls and Dad are outside on the patio with the kids, Henry and I walk back in and sit at the bar, ordering two beers. I have something I want to talk to him about.

"I guess you heard I quit my job."

"Yeah, bro, but I think you did the right thing. I could never work with someone like that."

"So, I was thinking... How would you feel about starting our own practice?"

"You know I would love that, Mitch, but there's no way I'm leaving Fayetteville. We love it here."

"I know. I'm not asking you to leave, Henry. What would you say if I said I wanted to move here?"

He blinks at me, as if he couldn't have heard me right. "I'd say that'd be *fucking* awesome. What does Jayna think about that?"

"I haven't said anything to her yet. I wanted to see what you

thought first. I really think she'd be more than happy to move, especially considering everything that has happened. She can get a job
anywhere."

"You know, if we open a private practice, we can handle a little
bit of everything. Your experience with divorce law and my business
and tax law experience will be a great combination."

I smile. "I haven't been this happy or excited about work in a long
time. I'll talk to Jayna tonight and see what she says." I reach out my
hand, giving my brother's a hearty shake.

We finish our beers and head back outside.

When I sit next to Jayna, she leans in and whispers, "Is everything okay? Y'all were inside for a long time."

I kiss her softly. "Everything is terrific. I just had something I
needed to discuss with him. I want to talk to you about it when we get
back to the house."

"Now I'm worried."

I chuckle. "Don't be. I have a feeling you will love what I'm going
to propose."

"I trust you." She looks back toward the building. "Now if our
food would just hurry up." I don't even try to stifle the laugh that falls
from my mouth. She has always been impatient.

Emily basks in all the praise from everyone. She still holds the
bouquet of flowers Dad gave her at the end of her performance.

"Em, you were a superstar up there. One day, I'll be asking for
your autograph."

"Stop teasing me, Mitch."

"I'm not, sweetheart. You were amazing."

She gets up and climbs into my lap, kissing my cheek. "I love you.
I won't even charge you for an autograph." The entire table bursts out
laughing.

Our food comes, and we all dig in. Michelle must love it because
she hasn't said more than a word or two, and that girl usually loves to
talk. She will make a good lawyer one day.

Once we're done, Dad pays for everyone's meal, even though we each want to pitch in.

I shake my head. "Dad, you know you don't have to pay for our meals anymore. You should let us pay for you and Marley."

"I'm your father, and it is my pleasure to pay for your meal."

Henry pipes in, "Just say thank you, Mitch, and stop the sap fest."

I pick up my napkin and throw it at him.

Jayna nudges me under the table. I look up in time to see Michelle do the same thing I just did. "Sorry," I whisper. "I'm going to have to get used to little eyes watching everything I do and ears hearing everything I say."

Henry joins in the game, throwing the napkin back at Michelle, who is quite pleased with herself.

Kristi gives Henry a knowing look. "That's the truth. You should see how much money I have in my swear jar." Henry looks at Mitch and shrugs.

After lunch, Kristi and Henry say their goodbyes and head home. Emily rides in the minivan with us. Both girls are asleep by the time we get to the house. Dad picks up Emily and carries her inside, while I bring in Michelle. Neither one of the girls wake up, so we carry them upstairs and put them down in Emily's bed.

Dad quietly shuts the door. "I'm proud of you, son. You are going to be an amazing father to that beautiful little girl."

"I sure hope so. I'd be lying if I said I wasn't terrified, then I think back to the example you were and know I can handle it."

"You boys and your wonderful mother made it easy. Henry told me what you two talked about. I want you to know that nothing would make me happier than having my entire family back here."

"Thanks, Dad. I'm going to go talk to Jayna about it now. Wish me luck."

He chuckles. "I don't think you'll need it. I have a good feeling about this.

"I think I'll ask Marley if she wants to lay down, too. That's what happens when you get old and have a young child. You take naps when they do."

I laugh. "You're not old, Dad." I waggle my brows. "I know what you and Marley are going to do."

He raises his eyebrows. "I'm not even going there with you, son."

When I come downstairs, Marley excuses herself, leaving me and Jayna alone.

"Okay, Mitch. You've made me wait long enough. What were you and Henry talking about?"

"I should make you wait longer." She shoots daggers at me. I hold up my hands. "I'm kidding."

"Spill it, mister."

"How would you feel about moving here? I talked to Henry about it, and we'd both like to open a private practice in Fayetteville. There's nothing holding us to Dallas. I will miss Luke, but knowing him, he'll follow me here." I snort. "Being a trust fund baby, he doesn't have to work. I know you like your co-workers, but you'd find a new job so easily. Hell, *you* could open a private practice right next to us."

Jayna smiles. "Wow. I don't think you even took time to breathe through that. Someone wants this pretty bad."

"I do, but if you say no, we'll stay in Dallas."

"I'd love nothing more than to move here. Michelle already loves it, and I think she'd be really sad if she couldn't see Emily every day." She smiles, taking a deep breath. "You know what? Let's do this. I'm sure the clinic won't be surprised when I give my notice. I'm just not sure about getting out of my lease. Although I'm in a very sought-after building, so if there's a waiting list, they may let me out of it."

I cradle her face in my hands and gently touch my lips to hers, deepening the kiss. This is officially the best weekend of my life. First, she agreed to be my wife. Second, I now have a daughter. Third, I will be back with my entire family and open my own business. Life is good.

"Baby, let me make love to you. You've made me the happiest man in the world."

She swallows, looking around. "Here? In your dad's house? Isn't that a little...creepy?"

"What do you think he and Marley are doing right now?" I say with a devilish grin.

She cringes. "You just *had* to go there, didn't you?"

"Well, they are, so they won't be worried about what we are doing. The girls are zonked out for at least another hour. I say we take advantage and work on that baby brother or sister Michelle was asking for."

"Really? Are you ready for a baby?"

"I'm ready for as many babies as you want to give me. You can stop taking the pill any time."

"Let's get married first, then I promise to throw them into the trash."

"Is tomorrow too soon to get married?"

She laughs, but the serious look on my face stops her cold. When you know what you want, why wait? I'm sure people will question why so soon, but those who know us know this has been over ten years in the making.

EPILOGUE

One Year Later
~Mitch~

I sit in my home office, a smile on my face as I look out the window, watching Jayna and Michelle play in the pool in our back yard. It's been a hot summer, but this will probably be the last week before we close down the pool for the year. The temperature is mild during the day, but cooling down at night.

Moving to Arkansas was the best decision for us. We were able to find a house and move in less than a month. Michelle is in the best preschool and has made a lot of friends. Jayna found a job at a practice that is made up solely of female physicians. As soon as things slow down for us, she plans on buying into the practice.

Davis and Davis Law has taken off. We have more business than we can handle. I've tried to convince Margaret to move to Arkansas and work for me. She and her husband are coming to visit soon.

I love being able to do a little bit of everything, not just divorces. But the best part is working alongside my brother. This has been our dream for as long as we can remember. I know Mom is happy in heaven seeing her boys working together.

I look at our wedding photo on my desk. It was a perfect December day, four months after our engagement. As hard as I tried to talk her into it, she refused to elope. Our wedding was simple and beautifully decorated with poinsettias, Christmas trees, and Christmas lights. My family all flew out to Cincinnati so we could get married in the small church Jayna grew up in. Henry was my best man, Luke my groomsman. Kristi was the maid of honor, and Michelle and Emily were bridesmaids *and* flower girls. Jayna looked stunning. I still lose my breath when I think back to seeing her walk down the aisle to "Bless The Broken Road" by Caleb and Kelsey. There wasn't a dry eye in the church.

Speaking of stunning... Jayna in a white, two-piece swimsuit, eight months pregnant with my son, takes it to a whole other level. We tossed her birth control pills in the trash the night before the wedding, and it didn't take us long to conceive. Jay Matthew Davis will be born in just over three weeks. Our life is about to change, but I can't wait. We are both thrilled to be having a son and that he and Henry's son, Benny, an eight-month-old bundle of joy, will be so close in age.

As Jayna and Michelle climb out of the pool, Jayna looks up, sees me in the window, and smiles. She bends down to Michelle and points at the window. Michelle looks up and comes running into the house.

"Daddy, you're home!"

"I sure am. It's five thirty. I promised I'd always try to be home by six. Go change out of your swimsuit and get ready for dinner. We are going to eat with Papaw and Nanna in just a little bit."

"Okay, Daddy. I love you." She runs back out

"I love you, too, sweet pea," I call after her.

Jayna comes in and sits in my lap, placing a kiss on my lips. "How was your day, handsome?"

"Good. Did you hear from the prosecutor today?"

"Yes. They don't need me to come and testify. They have more than enough evidence, with the phone records, photos that were found at both the office and his home, and video footage around my building to prove the stalking charges. Plus, three other women have come forward with similar stories. He is confident Preston will be convicted. It goes to trial in two weeks."

"Why didn't you call and tell me?"

"I just got off the phone with him less than an hour ago. I knew you would be home soon and wanted to share the news with you in person. Did I just hear you tell Michelle to get out of her swimsuit and dressed for dinner?" I nod. "That gives us…" She looks at her watch, "at least five minutes. Can you work your magic in that amount of time?" She stands, placing her hand on her waist, jutting out her hip, a suggestive look on her face.

"Is that a challenge?" I growl. I have my pants unbuckled and dick freed faster than she can say my name, then stride to the door to lock it. "Hands on my desk, ass out."

Jayna does as she's told, wiggling her ass. I skim my hands up her arms and down her sides. "God, you are so sexy. This is going to be fast, so hold on."

"That's how I want it, baby. I can never get enough of you, especially now that I'm pregnant."

Taking my dick in my hand, I run it along her wet folds, hitting her clit, causing her to moan out my name and pant in anticipation. "Get ready, baby." It's all the warning she gets before I slam into her.

"Yes… Oh, right there, Mitch."

"Fuck, baby. You feel so good."

I thrust hard a few times, my orgasm rushing through me. We explode at the same time, trying to muffle our cries. Just like every time we make love, she blows my mind.

Once our breathing calms, Jayna gives me a quick kiss and rushes out the door to get ready for dinner. I think I may chase after her and get into the shower with her.

Just as I start to stride out the door, I hear, "Daddy, where are you? I'm coming to find you." I smile, thankful that with the love of my family, I know I'll always be found.

The end

THANK YOU

Thank you so much for taking the time to read *Finding Mitch*.

I'd love to hear from you.

Contact Lynn
    Facebook: http://bit.ly/2XNoa3L
    Reader Group: http://bit.ly/2RYigKR
    BookBub: http://bit.ly/2XPxoAR
    Goodreads: http://bit.ly/2FmgJIB
    Newsletter: http://bit.ly/2RZt8bg
    Twitter: http://bit.ly/2FrmgNR
    Instagram: http://bit.ly/2FqWsld

More from Lynn Jaxon:
    Just As I Am
    More Than Just A Name

ACKNOWLEDGMENTS

My readers:

Thank you so much for taking a chance on me. I love you all, value your friendship and support. I will never forget it.

My family:

To my wonderful husband... Thank you for supporting and encouraging me, for allowing me to spend so many hours on my computer or with my head in a book, for supporting my passion for reading and writing. There are no words to describe how much you mean to me. You are my rock!

To my three wonderful children and two precious grandchildren... You are my world. Thank you for all your support.

To Mom and Dad... You have always supported my dreams, for which I am grateful.

To my extended family... Thank you for supporting me and not thinking I am crazy. I love you all so much.

Kaylee Ryan:

I will say this over and over again...Thank you for being such an amazing friend, for everything you have done and continue to do to support me. You are my glue, that's for sure! You rock! Love ya!

My beta team:

Amy, Jill, Belinda, Jamie, Amber, Kristi, Mom... Thank you so much for taking time out of your busy lives to read and give me input on this book. So many times you stopped what you were doing to help talk me off the ledge, giving me encouragement and feedback. I'm never letting you go!

My wonderful reader's group, Lynn Jaxon's Reader's Lounge:

Thank you for all your support, for helping spread the love, for your encouragement! You are amazing! Some of you ladies are with me every day, making me smile, and I want you to know how much I appreciate you.

My bloggers:

Thank you for sharing, reading, reviewing, and helping spread the word to this wonderful book community.

My editor, Kim Young:

Thank you for editing my book and making valuable suggestions. You and your red pen sure know how to work magic! You truly blew me away.

Love Affair With Fiction:

Thank you, Jill Sava, for doing such an amazing job on my cover reveal and release blitz. I could go on and on about how much you've done for me. You are a rock star!

All my love,

Lynn Jaxon